SLADE

BARRY CORD

G.K. Hall & Co. • Thorndike, Maine

Published in 1999 by arrangement with Golden West Literary Agency.

This book contains the complete text of the Western novel *Starlight Range*, by Barry Cord.

G.K. Hall Large Print Paperback Series.

The text of this Large Print edition is unabridged.
Other aspects of the book may vary from the original edition.

Set in 16 pt. Plantin by Warren S. Doersam.

Printed in the United States on permanent paper.

Library of Congress Cataloging in Publication Data

Cord, Barry, 1913–
    Slade / Barry Cord.
        p.   cm.
    ISBN 0-7838-8568-7 (lg. print : sc : alk. paper)
    1. Large type books. I. Title.
[PS3505.O6646S56   1999]
813′.54—dc21   99-13802

SLADE

Chapter One

The two dusty riders came down the narrow trail that dipped steeply to the canyon floor and emerged onto a more traveled road that threaded through the high-walled canyon. Here the older man reined in, his quick glance reaching along the trial, probing up into the cold gray hills.

"We've got at least an hour on him, Red," he grunted. He had a bony, grizzled face that revealed a thinning patience.

Red nodded indifferently. He was a slight, frail-looking youngster twenty years younger than his companion. Close-cropped red hair and a mass of freckles spattering his narrow face made him look even more boyish. Despite the rawness in the air, he wore only a threadbare brush jacket which did not hide the bone-handled .45 jutting from a thonged-down holster on his right hip.

The wind made a dismal sound in the darkening canyon. The older man sniffed and wiped his nose with the sleeve of his coat. He didn't feel well. His bones ached. He was irritable, and he wanted to get this job over with.

A half mile down the road into the canyon, a low-roofed adobe structure made a T against the trail. The corrals flanking the building were empty, but a smudge of gray smoke whipped back from a fieldstone chimney.

"We'll wait for him at the Murado House," the older man decided. "He'll stop there. Everybody comin' down this trail does."

Red nodded. "My turn this time, Joe," he said quickly. He let his tone ride high, making it a query. Red kowtowed to no one, but he had a cool respect for this slouch-shouldered man who packed two guns. Joe Yader, who had ridden under a different name in Missouri, was not a man to be taken lightly.

Joe gave him no answer. He was frowning, blowing on his gloved hands, trying to work warmth into his fingers. "Blast the judge an' his law," he grumbled. "If I had my way we'd have moved in on Starlight long ago."

He jerked his spotted gray into movement, the action putting a period to his sentence. Red kneed his cayuse alongside his partner.

Five minutes later they pulled up before the trail house. Joe slid stiffly out of saddle and stamped his feet on the frozen ground. He leveled his gaze across his empty saddle and studied the road that led back into the winter-hazed hills. As far as his eyes could reach he saw no movement.

"Take the cayuses into the shed behind the north wing," he told Red. "I'll have the drinks ready when you join me."

He waited a moment by the door, a lanky,

dour man with thinning brown hair and a face weathered to granite hardness by a thousand violent encounters. He cursed softly, thinking of the border sun and the way it felt hot against his back.

By god, he thought sourly, it's time to cut loose and drift south.

Joe Yader always felt like this when ice began forming along the edges of the creeks — when the cold winds started blowing down from the high Wyoming hills.

Opening the door, he stepped quickly inside, then closed it slowly, leaning his weight against the solid oak planking. He stood motionless, slouched like some sleepy, mangy cat, his yellow eyes ranging across the dim, untidy room that was bar and general store. The stillness annoyed him.

He knew Nick Pathias had seen them. No one came down *Los Perdidos* trail that Nick didn't see.

Movement at the greasy drapes shrouding a doorway behind the bar caught his attention. A Mexican woman, well past the age of flirtation, shoved a stolid, oily face into the room. Black eyes surveyed him in stony silence. Then the face withdrew.

Joe scuffed up to the short bar, toed a spittoon out of his way. Nick came through the drapes as Joe leaned an elbow on the counter. The Greek was a slovenly, slack-mouthed man, with a five-day beard and small black suspicious eyes. He

9

pulled a suspender over dirty long-johns.

"Yah," he greeted them. "Wasn't expectin' company this late in the day." He brought a bottle of whiskey onto the counter and reached under it for glasses. He poured and slid a glass to Joe.

"How're things in Badwater?"

Joe eyed him with bleary unfriendliness. "Bad as the drinking water," he said curtly. It was his stock reply to the question, but he was feeling poorly today and in no mood for banter.

Nick laughed to be sociable. He refilled Joe's glass. "Way I hear it," he smirked, "Starlight's due for a new owner any day now."

The cold stare in Joe's eyes stopped him. "You hear too much, Nick," the gunman said. "Let it stay between yore ears!"

Nick licked his thick lips. "Only makin' conversation," he muttered sullenly. He glanced up as Red came in, kicking the door shut behind him. The redhead moved with an insolence that grated on Nick. But the Greek kept his annoyance under leash. The Colt on Red's hip was a lot of gun for so frail-looking a youngster, but Nick wasn't fooled. Red Owens had killed his first man at fifteen.

Joe jerked his head sharply. "Come an' get it, kid," he growled. He turned his attention back to Nick. "We didn't drop in jest to drink yore cheap likker," he added grimly. "Yo're due to have another customer in about an hour. We want a few words with him."

10

Nick looked from Joe to Red, who was openly checking the loads in his Colt. The lanky man's meaning was plain.

"I don't want a body layin' around here," he complained sourly. "Darn ground's froze stiff." He made a short gesture with his right hand. "Why don't you fellows wait for him past the bend?"

Red's voice cut in with bleak directness. "It's cold out, Nick!"

"Well — we'll take him with us!" Joe snapped. He slid money on the counter and picked up the whiskey bottle by the neck. "Bring the glasses, Red. We'll wait for him in one of the back rooms!"

A road runner came around a trend in *Los Perdidos* trail. It stopped abruptly, one foot poised off the ground. Beadily it surveyed the horseman coming toward him, as if wanting to dispute his passage. Then, thinking better of it, it turned with a flirt of its tail and disappeared among the off-trail rocks.

Slade pulled up at the bend and leaned forward for a better look at the country ahead. The trail looped in a lazy S down the bare slope, and far down, in the canyon, he saw the smoke from the Murado House.

"Reckon we both can stand some grub," he muttered, scratching the base of the gelding's ear.

The roan's breath flared white, and he nodded

vigorous assent. The wind off the higher slopes pushed against Slade's back, the chill prying through his coat, reaching down his collar.

He had been riding since early morning, and the trail house in the canyon was the first sign of habitation he had run across. He settled back in the saddle and put his attention on his back trail. . . . He waited a long minute before the rider showed up, a tiny dot cresting the far hill.

"That hombre's sure persistent," he muttered. He slid his hand down over the cold stock of his Winchester, then thought better of it. No one knew he was headed for Starlight; the rider might be no more than a stranger who wanted company on the trail.

The roan danced sideways on the rutted road. Slade gave him his head. He had waited five years to kill a man; a few hours one way or the other mattered little now.

He rode down off the main slope, and his roving eyes picked up the narrow trail which joined it. Fresh horse droppings at the junction told him that at least one rider had come this way ahead of him. His glance moved on ahead, picked out the tracks of two riders, and lifted to the trail house.

Two men had ridden this way less than an hour ago, but he could see no horses at the tierack. He absorbed this fast, but gave no outward indication he was aware of it as he pulled the roan up at the Murado House.

Nick was wiping a wet spot on his counter

when Slade entered. The Greek stopped wiping and stared at the rangy man, his bland eyes showing little friendliness.

Slade thumbed his hat back from his forehead as he walked to the stove and warmed his hands. After a moment he loosened his coat. Nick's glance dropped to the .45 caliber Colt in the holster thonged-down on his left thigh.

Slade ambled over the bar. He seemed to favor his right leg a little.

"Too raw a day to drink alone," he remarked pleasantly. "Join me?"

Nick automatically set up two glasses. The man across the bar loomed up bigger than he had first appeared. A rangy man with a slight limp and an unsmiling face. An odd face, Nick thought. The right side seemed cold and stiff, and his right temple was generously sprinkled with white; the rest of his hair was black.

He caught the cold regard of those gun-metal blue eyes and nodded jerkily. "Can't stand the stuff myself," he said "You headed south?"

Slade shook his head. "Should be, I reckon." He had a quiet voice, but there was an iron quality in it, a grimness that had become part of the man. "I'm headed for Starlight Basin."

Involuntarily Nick jerked his eyes to the greasy curtains. It was a mistake which he knew Red and Joe immediately caught, and the back of his neck grew cold. He gulped his drink to cover his confusion.

"About twenty miles southwest of here," he

mumbled. "The canyon trail will lead you straight to Badwater. Town's on the rim of the Basin." He pushed a full shot toward Slade.

"That's rough country up there," he ventured.

Slade nodded. "So I hear." He downed his drink, eyeing with level amusement the faint disturbance behind the greasy drapes.

Nick hastily refilled both glasses. "On the house," he said generously. His nerves were on edge. Mentally he was damning Joe Yader and Red for choosing his place to ambush this man.

"You hiring out with Crescent — or Starlight?"

A ghost of a grin touched the left side of Slade's mouth. "Kinda lost the habit," he said, shaking his head. "Hiring out, I mean."

Through the dirty window Slade could see a tumbleweed rolling along the trail, kicked along by the icy wind.

He added dryly: "I'm just drifting through."

He waited with his back against the bar, feeling tension building up in the room. Finally he saw the rider who had been trailing him since morning framed by the window. The man looked tired. He was hunched way over on his limping horse's neck. A long slab of a man, range-garbed, a mackinaw hanging like a blanket from bony shoulders. He was not a young man.

Slade turned then and picked up his whiskey glass. Someone was waiting behind the draped doorway. Waiting for whom?

Nick had seen the man, too. The Greek had

14

his palms on the bar, a puzzled frown on his swarthy face.

In the momentary silence the jingle of riding gear, the creak of saddle leather, a man's muffled curse came to them. Slade moved his shoulders around as the man's boots thumped haltingly on the steps. The door swung open. Immediately the chill wind slipped inside, making itself felt against Slade's face.

The newcomer stood framed in the opening, doubled over as if he had a bad stomach-ache. A flat-crowned black hat partially blotted out a walrus-mustached face.

Shock went through Slade, like a wind rustling through a big pine. It was all of five years since he'd seen the man. But Ben Hobbs hadn't changed much.

Nick yelled sharply: "Close that door, man!"

The newcomer straightened. He kept his left hand pressed to his middle. Backing tiredly, he closed the door with his weight. He leaned back against the panels then, as if resting. His head came up, but his eyes were glazed; they tried to focus on Slade.

"Been tryin' to catch up with yuh all day," he said. His voice had a measured, forced quality. "Ran my bronc plumb into the ground —"

His eyes blinked as Joe Yader stepped through the curtains and came around the bar. He sighed. Defeat drew its harsh pattern on his weathered face.

The gunman ignored Slade. "You could have

saved yourself a lot of trouble the first time, Ben!" he said coldly. "Don't try to make that same mistake twice!"

Ben ran the rough palm of his right hand across his face, pushing his hat up from a shiny forehead. He seemed very tired. His eyes moved wearily to Slade; he blinked and put his hand to his eyes, as though he were seeing things.

"Joe," he said wearily, "I rode three hundred miles to prove a girl an' her three-year-old button are entitled to Starlight. If you had any decency —"

"Now ain't that too bad!" Yader cut in hoarsely. "The judge'll cry in his Scotch when I tell him."

Temper lifted the older man's shoulders. He dropped his left hand to his side, and Slade glimpsed the ugly brown stain above the man's brass belt buckle, the sticky dark smear across the man's calloused palm.

Joe sneered. "You ain't got a Chinaman's chance, Ben. But go ahead — make yore play!"

"I wouldn't push him," Slade said. His voice was quiet, but it reached out and jerked Joe around.

The anger in his face faded swiftly as Joe eyed the muzzle leveled at him. Slade was standing against the bar, and his gun was held below the level of the counter. . . . The man still hidden behind the drapes could not see it.

"I'm the nervous type," Slade said bleakly. "I can't stand gents who stand behind curtains."

His thumb was drawing back on the hammer. "Tell your sidekick he can come out now."

Yader had hooked the thumb of his right hand in his cartridge belt, and he didn't dare lift his arm. He kept his eyes on Slade's Colt. "Red," he called out in a thick voice, "come out here! This joker's got me covered!"

There was no response from behind the curtains. The silence was suddenly a ragged emptiness in which death waited.

"Red!" Yader snarled in sudden fear. "Don't be a fool! Come out!"

Ben broke the tension, deliberately inviting death. He heaved away from the door and clawed for his Colt.

The greasy curtains billowed outward as a close-held gun blasted through them. Ben fell to his knees.

Slade's Colt came up and around. Slugs tore through the drapes, shearing a horizontal pattern waist-high through them.

Yader was cursing Red as he reached for his guns. He curled his fingers around the cold butt, had them clear of leather when Slade's lead smashed into him. He fell back against the bar and was still cursing Red Owens as he died.

The redheaded gunslinger lurched through the drapes, his fingers clawing at them for support. He clung to them like a tired boy; then the cloth ripped away and dropped over him as he fell.

Slade eyed the two men silently before turning

17

his attention to Nick Pathias. The barman was crowding his back shelves.

"Friends of yours?"

Nick shook his head violently.

Slade turned to Ben. The old Starlight ramrod had a toughness that brought admiration to Slade's face.

"Should have waited for me —" Ben was saying. He was down on his hands and knees, head hanging. "All I wanted — give you this." He fumbled in his coat pocket for a long thick envelope, stained with blood. "Do me a — favor — big fella." His voice was a rasping whisper. "Give this to Arrant Canady — important that he —"

Slade knelt beside him "Ben," he said. "You remember me, Ben?"

But Hobbs was past hearing. "Get this to Canady —"

Slade caught him as he went limp. He eased the man down and stood beside him, hunkered on his boot heels, remembering the last time he had seen Ben Hobbs. Ben had worked for him, and he had no quarrel with his old foreman. . . .

He took the envelope Ben had tried to give him and got to his feet. Nick was staring at him, slack-mouthed.

Slade turned to the bar. "I was going to stay for supper," he growled, "but I've lost my appetite." He put his foot on the wobbly rail and reached for the bottle. "I'll warm up on this while you get somebody to take care of my cayuse."

Nick nodded. "Right away, mister. . . ."

An hour later Nick watched Slade ride down the canyon trail. Hobbs' body lay across the saddle of Joe Yader's gray. The rangy man had swapped Ben's lame mount for Yader's fresher animal, and Nick grinned maliciously as he watched them fade among the shadows.

He was thinking of what would happen when this man rode into Badwater leading a Crescent horse.

Chapter Two

Matt Kingston came to the door of the *Starlight Gazette* and watched the rider coming up the street. The stranger was riding a big roan gelding, and behind him, trailing on a lead rope, plodded a tired gray mare. A dead man hung belly down across her saddle.

Matt had never seen the rangy man before, but the gray mare and the body draped across the mare's saddle he recognized. The impact dropped the bottom out of the morning for him and put grayness in his lean face; his hands curled helplessly as he sagged momentarily against the door.

He had been on his way to the lunch room across the street for coffee to carry back to the shop. Now he stood there, his mission forgotten, unmindful of the chill wind sweeping past him into the room.

He swore. His voice was bitter, tired, resigned.

The clicking of type in the room behind stopped.

"Why, Matt!" a woman's voice scolded. Footsteps came up behind him and he turned quickly, trying to block her view of the pack animal just coming past the newspaper building.

"I just remembered something, Laura," he

invented swiftly: "that stick of type on the opening of the millinery shop. I've got a few corrections I wish to make —"

The woman's smiling gray-green eyes searched his face. "Such a weak excuse, Matt," she chided. "What is it you don't want me to see?" Her glance moved past him as she talked, a low cry escaping from her.

The morning sun laid its chill light down the wide, rutted road. The bitter wind, driving men indoors, left the road deserted so that rider and pack animal stood out boldly against the dismal building line.

The woman turned to the *Gazette* publisher. "Matt, that's Ben Hobbs!"

Matt took her arm. "Come inside, Laura," he said gently. "There's nothing we can do for Ben now."

The woman let herself be pulled back inside the office. Matt shut the door. He was a man ten years older than Laura, aged by the seriousness in his hazel eyes, the gray in his hair. A long-shanked, sinewy man who had found putting out a frontier-town newspaper less of a crusade than a hard and often thankless job. Some toughness of fiber kept him at it, even after the realization had been driven home to him that he'd never make much money at it and that there were easier ways of using his talents.

The woman moved away from him, stopping by the big stove that warmed the shop. She was on the tall side for a woman, slender, shapely;

21

and even with ink smudges on her cheek and a leather apron around her waist, she could take a man's attention and hold it.

Matt's fingers tightened helplessly. A year ago he had about given up the *Gazette* as a bad job and decided to move out of Badwater. That was shortly after Judge Selman had come to town and started to make a mockery of what little law had existed in Starlight Basin. When Matt's friend, Larry Brill, who had worn a marshal's badge in town, had been killed trying to restore order in one of the saloons and the new marshal had taken over, Matt had decided to clear out.

Then Laura Canady had showed up in Badwater, and he had changed his mind. Laura was Arrant Canady's daughter-in-law — a married woman with a three-year-old son. So she claimed, and Matt believed her. But Laura had been unable to prove that fact to the boss of Starlight. Old Arrant Canady had refused to believe that his only son, Philip, who had left home years before, was the kind of man who would desert a woman and his child.

This was the girl with whom Matt Kingston had fallen in love.

Her voice broke through his thoughts. "I didn't want Ben to go. But he believed in me, Matt. And he wanted to help young Tommy." Her voice trailed off in a tired whisper. "He rode all the way to Bisbee to get proof of my marriage. And they killed him for it."

Matt lifted his shoulders. "We can't beat

22

them, Laura. I can't fool myself any longer." He glanced out the window, discouragement pulling the corners of his mouth down so that he looked older. "With Ben gone, there's no one left at Starlight who can stop them. Crescent'll take over before the end of the month!"

His hands fumbled with the type cases. "Once, Laura," he mused bitterly, "long ago, I used to believe that the pen was mightier than the sword, that the truth could stop men like Judge Selman. I believed that a good newspaper stood between the law and the men who broke it — and that a newspaperman's job was to get the truth and report it so that honest men could judge accordingly. I believed this, Laura — until I came to Badwater."

He looked down at the lead slugs in his hand, not seeing them, but thinking of what he had expected the *Gazette* to be. In a burst of temper he hurled the slugs against the far wall.

The *Gazette*'s editor and publisher was not the only person who noticed Slade come to town. On the corner of Trail and Main Streets stood the Open House Bar, the biggest and most influential of Badwater's many saloons.

A stocky individual had just emerged from the place, stopping at the bottom of the stairs to pull up the collar of his coat. Slade's passage held his attention. His eyes followed Slade down the street; then, swearing softly, he turned to the stairs and took them three at a time.

Four hard-faced men were playing a desultory game of pinochle at a table. All eyes lifted to watch him run down the middle of the big room, past the sleepy-eyed bartender, to a rear door marked: JUDGE SELMAN, Private.

One of the players remarked dryly: "Wonder what's gotten into Dooley now?"

"The judge's errand boy," the man across from him sneered. "Me — I'll run for no man!"

Dooley heard neither of these remarks. He was in a hurry, and in his haste he nearly committed suicide.

He put his hand on the knob and was halfway inside the rear office before he remembered the cardinal rule the Judge had laid down — *no one entered without knocking!*

The slight, black-tailored, scholarly-looking man standing in front of the glass-enclosed bookcase had his back to the door. Dooley had this brief glimpse of the judge before the man whirled. A puff of smoke, flame-centered, blossomed from an under-arm holster.

Dooley gave a strangled cry and stumbled against the inner wall, clutching a torn left ear.

"You blundering idiot!" Selman's voice trembled with controlled rage. "Next time I'll put a half-ounce of lead in that thick skull!"

Dooley wagged his head, fear clogging his tongue. The curious faces of the card players appeared beyond the open door. The judge walked forward, dismissing them with a brief gesture, and closed the door.

"What brought you back?" Selman snapped. "I thought I told you to ride out to the ranch to find out if Red and Yader had come back?"

Dooley managed to put words together. "Judge — Ben Hobbs is back!"

Walter Selman, better known as Judge Selman, frowned. He was a medium-tall, extremely slender man of fifty, but he carried himself with a military erectness that gave people the illusion of greater height. He had a pale, transparent skin that didn't burn or darken, and the long iron-gray sideburns went with the air of solemn dignity he affected.

Selman had come to Badwater a year before with a battered suitcase, a copy of Blackstone, an expensive cigar, and an under-arm Smith & Wesson .38-caliber pistol which he could use with deadly efficiency. Behind him were years of varied occupations, including two years of on-the-job training with Quantrell's Raiders. The law was not unfamiliar to him; he had studied it and broken it with periodic frequency since he had run away from the Virginia Military Academy as a boy of fifteen.

He had little stability and no loyalty to anyone but the figure which looked back at him from a mirror; consequently he had never married. He had come to Badwater with some money and bought out a small spread called Crescent. Ownership gave him a stake in Starlight Basin and mock dignity to his role as self-styled arbiter of the law west of *Los Perdidos*.

Now he looked at his rider, his eyes narrowing in disapproval. "Well?"

Dooley was holding a dirty handkerchief to his bleeding ear. "Hobbs came into town across the saddle of Joe Yader's hammerhead gray mare," he mumbled. "But it wasn't Joe who brung him in," he added hastily. "It was some big jasper I never saw before."

"Where's Joe?"

Dooley shrugged. "But it was Joe's gray this jasper was leadin', Judge. An' it was Ben across the saddle."

Selman eased himself down into a chair behind the flat-topped mahogany desk. "A stranger to Badwater, you say? Leading Joe's horse?" A small, cruel smile tightened his lips. "Why, that's horse-stealing, wouldn't you say, Dooley?"

Dooley's eyes widened. "Yeah — it shore is."

The judge's smile grew wider. "Get the marshal. Tell Bill Talley I want that horse thief brought in here." He made a gesture toward the saloon. "How many of the boys are out there?"

"Pete, Hal, Teach an' Walleye," Dooley responded eagerly.

"Enough for a jury," Selman said softly. He leaned back in his chair and clasped his hands judiciously. "Dooley — inform the town marshal that court is now in session."

Slade read the sign painted across the curtained show window of the funeral parlor and

26

decided it would be a good idea to leave Hobbs here. Then he'd inform the local authorities and Canady, in that order, of what had happened at the Murado House. The decision brought him a bleak pleasure.

He turned the big roan into the alley flanking the building and dismounted by the side door of Josel's Funeral Parlor. His knock echoed in the alley.

He waited, a rangy man fashioning a cigaret, hunching against the raw wind to light up. He was taking his first puff when the door cracked open. A short, pudgy man with a fringe of white hair encircling the shiny bald crown of his head took in Slade's range-clad figure and mistook his needs.

He said sharply: "This is a funeral parlor, stranger. The nearest bar is two doors down."

Slade put his shoulder against the closing door. "I'll have a drink later," he said quietly. "Right now I want to leave a body with you."

The undertaker frowned. "Well —" His jaw dropped as he saw the dead man across the saddle of the slack-hipped gray. "Why — it's Ben Hobbs!"

Slade nodded. "He's dead."

The undertaker wagged his head. "Hobbs, too," he muttered. He stepped back into the room. "Bring him inside. Over here."

Slade carried Ben's body to a long wooden table in a corner of the room. Josel pulled a threadbare blanket over the dead man and turned to Slade.

"I understand Ben worked for the Starlight brand," Slade said; "for a man named Arrant Canady."

"Used to work for Canady," Josel corrected him stiffly. "Arrant Canady's dead, too."

Slade stared. Something in his face caused the undertaker to say: "Did you know Canady?"

He repeated the question. Slade shrugged. "Yeah." He turned slowly, like a man who had lost his way. At the door he paused, pulled himself together. He looked back at the undertaker, who was watching him with nervous anxiety.

"Just before he died Ben asked me to deliver something to Arrant Canady. That was only yesterday —"

The pudgy mortician rubbed his hands together in a nervous gesture. "I don't know where Hobbs has been. But Arrant Canady died last week. He'd been a semi-invalid for a year. His heart finally quit on him."

Slade thought: *It quit too soon.*

He stood by the door, feeling lost. The years of pain, of semi-paralysis marched through his thoughts. The years of grim, sustained effort of will, the determination to walk again, to come face to face with his old partner, Arrant Canady, had led to nothing.

By a matter of a few hours Arrant Canady had beaten him.

Josel said: "Will you be notifying the law about Ben, mister?"

Slade roused himself. "I'll see the sheriff," he nodded. "I'll explain how it happened."

He turned to the door, and the gun stopped him. It was a Navy model, .45-caliber, seven-inch barrel — and it looked like a toy gun in the palm of the biggest man Slade had ever seen!

"You'll tell me the story, fella," the man growled. "I'm Badwater's town marshal!"

Chapter Three

The man with the badge filled the entire doorway. He towered at least six feet five inches tall and looked four feet wide. He was wearing black pants that barely reached to the tops of his scuffed boots. A gray-and-black plaid wool shirt, unbuttoned at his thick neck, strained across his huge chest. On top of those massive shoulders his close-cropped bullet head seemed too small, almost ridiculously out of proportion.

Slade looked him up and down, wondering how so big a man had come through that doorway without making much sound.

"Is that all of you?" he murmured.

"Let's not be funny," the marshal warned. For so big a man he had a high, rather thin voice.

Slade shrugged. I didn't mean to be funny. Put away that Colt and I'll buy your coffee while I have breakfast. I'll tell you what happened to Ben Hobbs then."

"It ain't Hobbs I'm interested in," the marshal snapped. He was moving aside to let a man with a handkerchief tied around his head slip inside. The newcomer looked like a pygmy alongside the lawman.

"You work for Crescent?" the marshal said.

His voice held a thin sarcasm.

"No."

The huge lawman jerked a thumb to indicate the gray mare moving restlessly in the alley. "There's a Crescent brand on that cayuse, mister. That's a local brand. Now you tell me where you picked up that animal."

"At the Murado House, about twenty miles east of here," Slade replied grimly. "The man who owned her was through riding."

"Wal, now," the marshal drawled, "sounds like a clear case of hoss-stealin' to me. Dooley, get his iron." He sneered at Slade's tightening jaw. "Before you decide to commit suicide," he added contemptuously.

Dooley sidled around behind Slade. His hands moved swiftly, hefting the nicely balanced gun. He thrust it inside his belt and stepped back.

"The judge's waitin', Bill," he reminded the man eagerly.

"Wait a minute!" Slade protested. "Just because I brought a dead man to town on a Crescent horse —"

"Tell it to Judge Selman!" the marshal growled. "You'll get a fair trial an'," he grinned maliciously, "a quick execution!"

Slade glanced at Josel, wondering if this was some kind of gag Badwater played on strangers. But the pudgy undertaker didn't meet his eyes.

"What is this?" Slade snarled. "Some kind of joke?"

The huge marshal had walked up close; his gun muzzle was less than a foot from Slade's stomach.

"Why, sure, mister," he chuckled. "We don't mean nothin' —"

He batted his left hand into Slade's mouth. It was a fast move, and the open-handed cuff slammed Slade clear across the room. Slade bounced off the wall and almost fell. He caught hold of a table and steadied himself, feeling blood on his lips, warm and salty. He looked up and saw the massive figure of the marshal through the red haze of anger.

He lunged for the man.

Dooley thrust his foot out, and Slade stumbled. The marshal was still chuckling as he brought his right arm down in a cuff across Slade's head.

Slade went down and rolled over. The glancing blow had cleared his head somewhat. It had also served to channel his driving rage. He pulled himself up along the leg of the table that held Hobbs' body, and when he turned to face the marshal there was a crooked smile on his lips.

"I can bounce you around some more," the lawman sneered. "But if you've got enough, we'll get moving. I don't like to keep the judge waiting."

Slade pushed away from the table. He moved out through the door ahead of the marshal. His roan was waiting for him. Slade stopped. Talley shoved him half-way across the alley. "Keep moving!"

Dooley paused in the doorway. "That's a lot of hoss, Bill," he said. "Joe's gray mare looks like a scrub beside him."

The marshal shrugged. "Impound him."

Slade kept walking. He turned right at the corner at the lawman's growled instructions, and with every step his anger grew until it fretted against his nerves with increasing pressure.

Faces appeared in windows as he was marched down the street. They walked past the *Gazette* windows, and out of the corner of his eye Slade noticed a tall, spare man and a woman in the doorway.

Behind him Marshal Talley's voice squeaked: "Here's news for that weekly sheet of yores, Matt. This is the hoss thief that killed Ben Hobbs. I'm taking him to court to stand trial now."

Matt's voice was stiff with sarcasm. "Perhaps the town should vote you a raise for such diligence to duty, Talley."

The marshall paused. "Mebbe I ain't up on them dictionary words, Matt," he warned softly. "But one day I might find it my duty to take your place apart — an' you with it. Keep that in mind, fella!"

Matt's eyes were thoughtful as he watched Talley and his prisoner move down the walk. Beside him Laura said: "It doesn't make sense, does it? If he had killed Ben, why would he have

33

brought his body to town?"

"I don't know," Matt replied. "But for once I'm going to attend one of Judge Selman's mock trials."

Laura's fingers tightened on his arm. "Matt, don't get mixed up in this. You heard Talley. They're just waiting for an excuse to get you."

"I'll keep out of trouble," he promised. "But I've got a strange feeling that this trial isn't going to come off like all the others they've held in the Open House." He turned his glance down the street to where Slade and the marshall were just mounting the saloon steps.

Gently he pushed the woman back inside the shop. "It's been a long time since I've had a decent story for page one. I think I'm going to have one today; a story I've been waiting a year to write."

The judge's court was in session when Slade entered the Open House. Selman was seated behind a small table which had been placed by the end of the bar.

Four of his riders were lined up along the brass rail. A scant dozen townsmen had drifted in to see the show. Most of them were shiftless hanger-ons in Badwater, who cared less for the principles involved than for the spectacle of a stranger being railroaded. These were lined up against the far wall.

Clustered around the staircase leading to

34

upstairs rooms were the entertainers of the gambling house.

The marshal stopped with Slade in front of the judge's table.

"Yore Honor," he said smugly, "here's the polecat who killed Ben Hobbs."

Slade glanced down at the figure behind the table. He saw a scholarly-looking man whose pale hands moved restlessly on the table top, his fingers moving as though along a piano keyboard. The man's black cutaway coat lent an air of judiciousness that was belied by the crude mockery of the proceedings.

The judge's eyes met Slade's stare. "This is a court of law, stranger," he pointed out with cold authority, "the only law this side of *Los Perdidos*. You'll get a fair trial here — and a quick one."

He let his statement rest, and shifted his weight on his chair. An eyebrow cocked at Slade's unblinking regard.

"Your name?"

"Smith." Slade's voice was cold, direct and grim. The blood on his cut lips had vanished, but not the anger at the manhandling he had received from the law in Badwater.

Judge Selman's eyebrows lifted in disbelief. "Mr. Smith," he continued smoothly, "do you plead guilty or not guilty?"

"Of what?"

"Of the charges brought against you!" Judge Selman snapped. "Of killing a man named Ben Hobbs and stealing a Crescent horse!"

Selman glanced at the marshal's scowling face. "According to witnesses, you arrived in town with Hobbs' body across the saddle of a gray mare bearing a Crescent brand. For your information, and entirely irrelevant to this issue, Mr. Smith, that brand belongs to me. I don't know how you came into possession of that animal. But under the circumstances, the evidence is conclusive. In front of this court you are charged with murder and horse stealing."

Slade's glance appraised the four men lined up along the bar: hard, gun-hung individuals placed there more to back any sentence the judge might hand out than to weigh the merits of the case before it.

Slade thought swiftly. No one in Badwater could know who he was or why he had come here. By this phoney jurist's admission, the two men he had killed in the Murado House had been in his employ. The letter they had obviously been after was in his coat pocket, but Selman couldn't know this. Nor could anyone now in Badwater know what had happened at the trail house.

He might have a chance to bluff this out.

"Just a minute, Judge," he said. "How do you know that Ben Hobbs wasn't dead when I found him? It could be that I was headed this way for a job with Crescent. I might have mistaken Hobbs for a Crescent rider — he was riding a Crescent horse — and bringing him to Badwater might have appeared like a good way to get hired by

Crescent's boss."

He saw doubt glitter briefly in the judge's pale eyes, and a grudging admiration twisted the man's lips. Slade was banking on the fact that Hobbs' death meant little to this man and that the trial had been arranged chiefly to force information from him. If this were so, his indication that he had been on his way to apply for work with Crescent should appeal to the man.

Selman looked pointedly at the town marshal. "Bill — did you see this man riding Joe Yader's mare?"

The huge lawman scowled. "No."

The judge's lips held an amused quirk as he turned his attention to Slade. "In view of the fact that the evidence against you, on both charges, is purely circumstantial in nature, I fine you fifty dollars. Pay now." He leaned back, waited a moment, and then added in a tone audible only to Slade, "And see me in my office about that job."

Slade hesitated. "Why the fine if I'm not guilty?"

Selman's thin smile faded. "That fine is now one hundred dollars," he snapped, "for contempt of this court!"

Slade checked the quick surge of anger. He pulled out a small roll of bills from his pants pockets, counted them, dropped them on the table in front of the self-appointed judge.

"Sixty dollars," he said flatly. "All I have."

The judge lifted his eyes to the marshal. "Give

him five days in jail, Bill." He turned his attention to Slade. "If you still want to work for Crescent when you get out, come around and see me."

He picked up the money, stuffed the bills in his vest pocket, and got to his feet.

"Court is dismissed!" He turned without another glance at the prisoner and joined the four grinning men at the bar.

The marshal nudged Slade. "You heard the verdict," he growled. "You got off easy, Smith."

"Glad you think so, Marshal." Slade's voice was dry, but a cold rage danced just below the glitter in his eyes. He could hear a man running up the street, his boots pounding on the hard ground. Men near the door were turning expectantly.

The lawman gave Slade a hard shove. "On yore way, Smith!" he growled. He had his huge hand on the butt of his Colt. "Let's get out of—"

He hesitated as the running man turned up the saloon steps. The man stumbled, fell against the batwings. They banged against the inner wall, sounding a jarring note in the stillness.

Dooley lurched to a halt. The Crescent man was bleeding from an ugly gash in his head. Part of his scalp hung grotesquely over his right eye. His left arm hung limply at his side.

"That blasted roan!" His voice was shaken, wild. "Turned on me, Bill! Near killed me —"

For a bare moment Big Bill's eyes left Slade. And in that instant Slade hit him.

Slade's fist sank wrist deep in the town marshal's stomach. Talley's breath wheezed out in one choking gasp. He gagged. His knees buckled. He tried to draw his big Colt. Slade jammed his shoulder into Talley's side, quartering the huge man around. Talley's gun cleared leather. Numbed reflexes triggered a shot into the floor.

Slade jammed the heel of his hand contemptuously into the big man's face, almost snapping the lawman's head off. The man staggered, and Slade twisted the gun out of his hand and laid it in a savage swipe across Big Bill Talley's skull.

The town marshal went down like a giant redwood.

Slade whirled away from the fallen marshal, the lawman's Colt in his hand, and made a slow survey of the surprised gunmen along the bar. Over that rock-steady muzzle a pair of cold and wicked eyes marked them, one by one.

"Let's call this court into session again, shall we?"

No one moved. Judge Selman had his back to Slade; he was watching his erstwhile prisoner through the bar mirror. The men ranged alongside him were partially faced around; they were debating the wisdom of challenging the grim-faced man holding the marshal's gun.

Slade gestured to Dooley, who was standing dazedly looking down at Big Bill Talley. "Come here!"

"What happened to my cayuse?" Slade's voice was ominous.

Dooley wiped blood from his face. "Turned on me while I was leadin' him an' the gray to the stables." He shrank back at the look in Slade's eyes. "I didn't hurt him, fella. He got away. Headed out of town, down the south trail."

Slade let out a slow breath between clenched teeth. "Lucky he didn't kill you!" he said coldly.

Dooley still had Slade's .45 in his waistband. Slade relieved him of it, slipping it back into his empty holster. He kept Talley's big Colt in his hand for arguing purposes.

He gave Dooley a shove toward the bar. He followed behind the hurt man, stopped at the table where the judge had held court.

"Looks like there's been a mistrial," he said easily. "I rule that my recent fine was illegal and thereby unjustified. I'll take back my sixty dollars!"

Selman didn't turn around. In the mirror Slade could see the stillness in the man's face, the blankness in his eyes. Temper spurred hard through Slade. This man had rigged this mock trial in which he was to have played the buffoon; now it was turnabout.

Impulsively he laid the marshal's Colt down on the table, pushed it toward Selman's back, and stepped away, his hands now empty, hanging loosely by his sides.

"You've had your fun, playing judge and

jury," he bit out. "Here's your chance to be executioner, Judge!"

Selman's thin shoulders twitched. But it was the tall, tow-haired hardcase standing beside Crescent's boss who accepted Slade's challenge. He whirled, his right hand flipping up his Colt.

Slade drew and fired. Teach jerked violently to the impact of lead. He slid along the polished bar into Selman, who didn't move. The gunman's knees buckled, and he fell limply across the shiny rail.

Without being told, Dooley and the others at the bar raised their hands high.

Slade's voice held no compromise. "Judge — the sixty dollars!"

Selman turned, stepping over Teach's body. He walked to the table, avoided Talley's Colt, and very carefully placed Slade's money on the table.

Slade picked up the money with his right hand, thrust it into his pocket without counting it.

"I expect to be in town for a while," he said. "If you're still in the mood for hiring, look me up. I might consider it."

He stepped back, his eyes holding the men at the bar. No one moved. The spectators nearest the door edged away as Slade headed in that direction. No one stirred for a full minute after the doors quit swinging behind him.

Judge Selman made the first move. He raised his foot and jammed his instep against the edge

41

of the small table, sending it skidding toward the doors. His voice held a suppressed fury.

"Clear the house!"

He waited, a small, deadly figure gripped by a grim frustrated anger, until only Dooley, sagging in sick pain against the bar, and the three Crescent gunmen remained. The girls had gone back upstairs.

Slowly he got control of himself.

"Pete! Ride back to the ranch. Saddle the best horse we got, get cookie to give you grub for a week. I want you to back-track this Smith hard-case all the way back past *Los Perdidos* if you have to. Don't come back until you find out who he is, and what happened to Joe Yader and Red Owens. Savvy?"

Pete Cajun, half Crow Indian, nodded silently. He looked down at Teach, his black eyes glittering. "Me find," he grunted.

Selman jerked a thumb toward Talley. The marshal was stirring, shaking his head like some stricken St. Bernard. "Get him up to the bar. But handle him easy. Big Bill's going to have a bad head for a day or two — a real bad head."

Chapter Four

Slade was finishing his dinner at Ma Crane's Kitchen, a small, neat lunch room across the street from the Stage Hotel, when a small voice piped from behind him: "Stick 'em up, mister!"

Slade turned on his stool and slowly raised his hands. A look of grave concern crossed his face. His glance dropped to the shiny badge on the calfskin vest.

"Sorry, Sheriff," he apologized meekly. "You've got me —"

"Bang! Bang! You're dead!" The small voice was gleeful. "Fall down, mister," it instructed.

Slade slowly brought down his hands, a smile tugging the left side of his mouth. "You sure don't believe in giving a hombre a break," he murmured. He swung off the stool and hunkered beside a solemn-faced boy who was holding a Smith & Wesson .38 in both hands. The gun's revolving chamber had been removed, rendering the weapon quite harmless.

"You're dead!" the boy repeated stubbornly. He was a wiry, sandy-haired fellow about three years old.

"Tommy!" Ma Crane came out of her kitchen, wiping both hands in her apron. "How many times have I told you not to aim that gun at people?" She turned to confront the lanky, leathery-faced man who came loping behind him. The man was puffing.

The boy's face lighted up. "Beat you, Hank!" he chanted gleefully. "Beat you!"

"Hank Emery!" Ma Crane's voice was harsh. "I distinctly recollect telling you to hide that gun from the boy!"

"Aw, Ma," the man protested, "Tommy can't hurt anybody with it. An' how's a button gonna learn to handle a hogleg if he don't start in early?"

"Humph!" Ma Crane turned to Slade, who had settled back on his stool. Her sharp eyes swept disapprovingly down that rangy frame, and her mouth pinched at the sight of the gun in the holster at his left hip.

Slade said: "He must be a handful, ma'am. If I had a boy like —"

"He ain't mine," the woman cut in sharply. But her voice softened as she looked at the boy who had backed into the protective custody of Hank's long legs. "His mother works for the *Gazette*, across the street. I take care of him during her working hours."

Hank was staring at Slade. "Say," he muttered, "ain't you the stranger Big Bill marched up to Judge Selman's court? The gent who turned the tables on that phoney law-an'-order bunch in the Open House?"

Slade nodded. "I was involved in a bit of legal misunderstanding," he admitted.

44

Hank's weather-beaten face lighted up. "Legal misunderstandin', yuh call it?" He grinned broadly. "Way I heard the story, you floored Big Bill, a feat nobody around here has even tried. You outshot Teach, one of the fastest gunhands in the Basin. An' yuh made Judge Selman back down in his own court!" Hank shook his head. "An' yuh call it a bit of legal misunderstandin'."

He stepped forward, thrust out a horny hand. "I don't know you, feller. But I'd take it as a real privilege to shake yore hand."

"Me, too," the youngster said gravely, extending a small fist.

Slade shook hands. Ma Crane came up behind the boy. "Tommy Canady," she said determinedly, "you run along into the kitchen. You, too, Hank!" she snapped. "The dishes are piling up, and we'll be having the dinner crowd on us in less than half an hour."

She turned to Slade, eyeing him with shrewd appraisal. "I took you for another Crescent hardcase," she admitted. "But if what Hank just said is true, the Lord help you. The quicker you leave Badwater, the healthier you'll remain."

Slade shrugged. "I'm particular about my health," he agreed. "But I came to the Basin on business. I spent five years planning it, ma'am. Got real set on it —" His eyes had a somber cast. He glanced toward the kitchen where Tommy's childish voice raised in sudden laughter. "Heard you call the younker Tommy Canady. I thought

45

the Canadys owned a big spread in Starlight Basin."

Ma Crane nodded. "Starlight's south of here, about seven miles out of town. Arrant Canady owned it, lock, stock and barrel. He died last week of a bad heart." Her lips pursed disapprovingly and she put her hands on her bulging hips. "And if you're wondering why Tommy is in my care while his mother earns a living working for Matt Kingston, it's because Arrant was an old moss-backed, mule-headed son who couldn't see the front of his nose if —"

She paused for breath. "Not that I want to run the man down after he's passed away, Lord rest his soul," she continued. "But if Arrant Canady hadn't been such a stubborn old fool, young Tommy and his mother would be at Starlight now, where they belong."

Slade's smile held little humor.

Ma Crane frowned. "Did you know Arrant Canady?"

"My business was with Arrant," he admitted.

She looked him over, trying to fathom what lay behind the small and mirthless smile. "You one of his old Montana hands?"

"I wouldn't say that," Slade replied. His voice held no emotion. "Was Canady from Montana?"

"He was. Thought you might be one of his old hands, seeing as how you said you had business with him."

"It wasn't that kind of business," Slade said.

Ma Crane gave a little shrug. "Arrant Canady came down here from Montana four years ago. Had a passel of money, a big herd, and troubles he wanted to forget. Found the Basin to his liking and settled here." The woman glanced out through her window. "It was Starlight that built this town. There wasn't but a few shacks squatting around the two bad springs before Canady drove his beef onto Basin grass. It was Starlight money and trade that built the whistle stop town of Siding, on the T & P spur track about ten miles east of here."

The woman wagged her head. "Not that I'm wasting any sympathy on him," she continued. "But Arrant Canady worked himself to death building Starlight up from scratch. The only hand he brought with him from Montana was his old foreman, Ben Hobbs. Rest of his riders he hired here."

"Who's running Starlight now?"

Ma Crane shook her apron at a lop-eared tomcat who came around the counter. "Scat! you good-for-nothing scavenger." She turned to Slade. "You'll have to ask Dr. Mays about that. Mays was the only friend Canady had in town. When he died he left Starlight in trust with the doctor." She brushed a damp strand of gray hair back from her face. "I think the old fool still expected his son to show up and take over at the ranch."

Slade was frowning. "Where does Tommy fit into this picture?"

"Tommy? He's Philip Canady's son, Arrant Canady's grandson —"

"I didn't know Philip Canady was married." Slade was reaching back in his memory, probing under the bitter layers of hate.

"He was married all right. He ran away from home about five years ago. That was on the old Montana ranch — the Pitchfork, I understand. He met Laura Mason, Tommy's mother, in Bisbee. But Philip Canady was not the paternal type. He walked out on her a month before Tommy was born. Laura waited for him to come back. She scraped along as best as she could before finally writing to Tommy's grandfather in Montana. She received word that Arrant Canady had moved down here. She thought Arrant might want to see his grandchild, so she packed her things and came to Badwater. She had her marriage license to Philip to prove she was his wife; nothing more. Someone stole it from her room the first night she put up here, at the Stage Hotel."

Hank's voice interrupted, calling for help from the kitchen.

The woman excused herself. "That fossil wouldn't find his head if it wasn't strung to his neck."

Slade remained on his stool. He was trying to reconstruct Philip Canady in his mind . . . a weak, spoiled boy with whom he had had little patience. He and Arrant had almost come to blows over the arrogant, wilful youngster who had spent more time in Ed Cavanaugh's gambling house than on the ranch. Philip Canady was what had finally broken an association that had started with good feeling; the old Pitchfork had been as much his as Canady's.

It had come to the point where old Arrant Canady had been faced with a choice of going along with his son or with his partner. Still, a bullet in the back was a hard way to terminate a partnership.

For almost a year Slade had lain paralyzed in an old sheepherder's camp. The Mexican doctor of sorts who attended him never expected him to move again. It took him a lot longer to get back his strength, his coordination. Some of the muscles on his right side would never move again. . . . It had taken months and a grim perseverance to shift from the natural use of his right hand and to acquire dexterity with his left.

Arrant Canady had left Montana after selling Pitchfork. But Starlight had been built up with Pitchfork money, and half of Pitchfork had belonged to Slade. He was almost thirty years old and had nothing to show for the long years which had passed. . . . It occurred to him that it would be hard to lay legal claim to this ranch Arrant Canady had left behind.

By law Starlight belonged to Arrant's son, Philip, if he could be found; or to Philip's wife, if she could prove her marriage. . . .

The recollection of Ben's old face, touched with the pallor of death, reminded him of the envelope in his pocket. He took it out and used his counter knife to slit it open.

The enclosure was a certified copy attesting to the fact that one Philip Canady had married Laura Mason on June 11, 1878 —

He heard the harsh scraping of a man's boots on the sill. Then a quiet voice said: "I saw you kill Teach, Smith. But this gun's already leveled at you — and not even the devil himself could beat the squeeze of my trigger finger!"

Slade's eyes came up to look at the man framed in the doorway. He was a tall, serious-faced man in his middle thirties, dressed in town clothes. He didn't look like a man used to settling arguments with a gun.

"What's on your mind?" Slade asked him coldly.

"Ben Hobbs!" the other answered. He heeled the door shut and walked to Slade, holding the short-barreled Colt very tightly in his fist. "Judge Selman didn't care what had happened to Ben," he said angrily, "but I do. I want to know how Ben died. Who killed him?"

Slade was trying to place this grim-faced man; now he remembered him standing in the doorway of the *Gazette*, watching, when Bill Talley had marched Slade to the Open House.

"Is this the way you round up news for your paper? At gun point?"

"Most of the news around here is made at gun point!" Matt snapped. "I'm writing Ben's obituary, and I want to know the name of the

50

skunk who killed him!"

Slade's eyes held a wintry stare. "Badwater seems to be made up of gun-itchy hands," he observed dryly. "Put that Colt away, and maybe I'll tell you who killed Ben Hobbs."

"You'll tell me now!" Matt snarled. "And I —"

"Matt!" Ma Crane's voice was alarmed. "Have you gone crazy?"

"Yeah!" Matt said bitterly, lifting his gaze to the woman who had come to the kitchen doorway. "Plumb crazy. Ben Hobbs is dead. This is the man who brought his body into town —"

"What does that prove?" Slade demanded grimly.

"You tell me!" Matt said. His eyes were hard, alert and hostile.

Slade was still holding Hobbs' bloodstained envelope between his fingers. Now he let it slip to the floor.

Despite himself Matt's eyes followed it for a fraction of a second. And in that instant Slade's right hand brushed Matt's Colt aside and his own .45 made a magic appearance, its muzzle nudging Matt's belt.

"Drop it!" Slade ordered crisply.

Matt dropped his weapon. He stared in harsh disbelief at the gun in Slade's hand. His breath came sharp between his teeth.

"Next time you aim a gun at a man, don't stand and palaver with him," Slade advised. "When you get that far — shoot!"

Matt's bitter glance dropped to Slade's leveled Colt. "Maybe you'd better take your own advice, Smith."

Ma Crane came between them, pushing Matt back, turning on Slade. "I'll have no trouble in my place, mister —"

"Smith," Slade said flatly. He shoved his Colt into his holster, bent to pick up Matt's gun and the envelope he had dropped. He slid the letter into his pocket and handed Matt his weapon.

"Put it away," he said coldly. "And stick to the business you know."

Matt flushed. Ma Crane said, flustered: "He's right, Matt. You had no right to come in here like that. If he had been one of Crescent's riders, you might not have gotten off so easily."

Matt stood his ground. A dogged determination to finish what he had come to do stiffened the back of his neck.

"I'm still asking about Ben Hobbs, Smith. He was a friend of mine. I want to know who killed him."

Slade was eyeing the gun in Matt's hand with a narrow regard; Matt shoved it in his pocket. "That's better," Slade said softly. "I got a bad impression of Badwater, mister. I wasn't here five minutes before the town marshal stuck his Colt under my nose —"

"I'm still asking you about Ben Hobbs," Matt cut in bitterly. "I don't give a hang about how you feel about this town."

Slade smiled bleakly. "You're not out to win

friends, either, I see." He shrugged. "Ben Hobbs was killed by a redheaded gunslinger name of Red Owens. He and another jasper I heard called Joe Yader were waiting for Ben in the Murado House. That's about twenty miles —"

"I know where that owlhoot road house is," Matt cut in impatiently.

"I happened to be there when it took place," Slade finished.

Matt frowned. Ma Crane had taken a seat and was listening, her face flushed from kitchen heat.

"You came into town leading Joe Yader's gray mare," Matt said. "What happened to Joe and Red?"

"They're dead."

Matt absorbed this, his eyes widening. "Then you —"

"I was caught in the middle," Slade said. "I had nothing against Crescent — until a few minutes ago."

Matt eyed him with an indecisive stare. He didn't like this man; there was a reserve about him, and a competence, that disturbed him. Ben had been Laura's last hope —

"Did Ben Hobbs have anything on him? An envelope?"

Slade stared impassively. Arrant Canady was dead, and Starlight belonged to Arrant's only offspring, Philip Canady. But Philip Canady was probably dead, too. That left Philip's wife — and her legal claim to Starlight lay inside the envelope in his pocket.

Why should she inherit Starlight? By rights the big ranch Canady had built up here belonged to him — at least half of it did. He had paid a bitter price for it. And he was in no mood at this moment to give it up.

"No," he said flatly. "I didn't find anything in Ben Hobb's pockets."

"Did you search him?"

"No."

"Then maybe I'm not too late," Matt said bitterly, "although I probably won't be the first to search a dead man's pockets."

Chapter Five

Dr. Jeffrey Mays was a slight, sallow-faced man in his late fifties. He had come to Badwater shortly after Arrant Canady had settled in the Basin, a thin-lipped solitary man driving a wagon that was both pharmacy and mobile medical office. He'd stopped for a drink in one of the saloons crowding Trail Street, and the drink stretched out into a week's binge.

When he came to he was in an alley, dirty, unshaven and with the shakes. He had been cleaned out of the several hundred dollars he still had on him, and his wagon, which he had left hitched in front of the saloon, was gone.

Sick and bitter, he had walked into the town marshal's office and delivered a verbal tirade to the two surprised men occupying it. One of those men had been Arrant Canady.

Both men had listened patiently. Then, when Mays had paused for breath, sinking onto a bench to steady his shaking knees, Marshal Brill had looked at the Starlight boss, and both men had uttered the same question simultaneously: "Do you play chess, Doc?"

At the time it had seemed such a silly question to the trembling, discouraged doctor that it had left him speechless. He'd merely nodded. And out of that had developed the new pattern of his life. Backed by Canady, he had put out his shingle and settled down to take care of Starlight Basin's medical troubles. . . .

He was in the Ace High Saloon, drinking alone at the end of the bar, a half empty bottle of whiskey at his elbow, when Slade found him. A moody man, Mays had taken to drinking again after Marshal Brill and Canady had died.

Slade walked up to him, ignoring the stares of the others in the bar. He said: "Dr. Mays?"

The slight man gave him a sour glance. "I'm on vacation," he growled. "Sign on my door — no patients until next Tuesday."

"I saw the sign," Slade said. He shook his head at the bartender who was approaching them. "Doc — I want to have a talk with you."

Mays waved a trembling hand. "Some other time, fella —"

"It won't keep that long," Slade interrupted. His voice was impatient. "I want to talk to you about Starlight."

Dr. Mays squinted at him. There was a pain over his eyes that bothered him, and his stomach was on the verge of nausea. He should let up, he thought dismally — but there was only the prospect of dull routine ahead of him, and he did not feel up to it.

"Who are you?"

"Name's Gil Slade," the other said shortly. "Name probably doesn't mean anything to you, but —"

"Slade?" Doc Mays straightened. He peered at Slade as through a haze, shook his head and ran trembling fingers through spare pepper-shot hair. "Gilbert Slade of Montana?"

Slade nodded, hiding his surprise behind a remote and stony stare.

Mays let out a slow breath. "We'll talk in my office, Mr. Slade." He dug in his vest pocket for money, tossed it on the bar, and picked up the whiskey bottle by the neck.

"I've been expecting you to show up, Slade," he said. "Waited for six months —"

Slade followed him out and down the street into the next block and up a flight of stairs into a sparsely furnished room. Dr. Mays walked to a washstand, splashed water over his face and dried himself on a towel. He seemed a bit more sprightly when he turned to face Slade.

"Sit down," he invited. He found two glasses and placed them beside the whiskey bottle on the small table. "Canady waited a long time for you to show up."

Slade frowned. "For me?"

Mays shrugged. "If you're Gilbert Slade." He sank into a leather chair and leaned back and closed his eyes. "He didn't tell me much about you; just that he expected a man named Gilbert Slade to show up at Starlight, asking for him. He was waiting for you — up to the last. When he knew he was dying, he had me and Frank Lawson in to witness his will —"

Slade's smile held incredulity.

Dr. Mays looked up at him. "He left half of Starlight to you, Slade, in case you ever showed up here. The other half goes to his son, Philip, or whatever heirs Philip left."

Slade walked to the desk, picked up the whiskey bottle and poured. He held the drink in his hand, his eyes somber, as if trying to read the past in it.

"I left Arch Nelson in charge at Starlight," Mays went on, "until Ben Hobbs got back from Bisbee —"

"Ben Hobbs is dead," Slade cut in. His voice held a flat bitterness.

"Ben?" Mays got to his feet and joined Slade at the table. He picked up the bottle, poured himself a drink and downed it in one gulp. He shuddered and wiped his mouth with the back of his hand.

"There's no one left, then." He turned to Slade, "You do have identification?"

Slade reached in his coat pocket for his billfold. He still had his old Army discharge, folded and worn, but readable. Mays glanced at it and handed it back.

"Good enough for me, Slade."

"What about Philip Canady?"

"He's probably dead," Mays said. "Arrant tried for years to locate him. I think he put notices in all the papers in the country. If Philip read any of them, he ignored them."

"I understand Philip married," Slade said.

Mays nodded. "Laura Canady and her son

58

showed up here a couple of months ago. She claimed to be Philip Canady's wife, but she had nothing to prove it. She told a story about having her marriage license stolen the first night she came here. She had taken a room at the Stage Hotel." Mays walked back to his chair. "Arrant was cagey. He had never given up hope his son would come home. He found it hard to believe that Philip could desert his wife and young son. But Ben Hobbs believed her. He took it upon himself to ride to Bisbee to get a copy of her marriage license —"

He got up again and walked to the window and opened it. He felt pretty bad. The cold wind blew into the room. Slade waited. Dr. Mays looked like a derelict, with shaggy hair creeping down his collar.

After a spell Mays wheeled away from the window. "You say Ben Hobbs is dead? How did he die?"

Slade told him what had happened in the Murado House. He took the envelope from his pocket and handed it to Mays.

"I had known Ben back in Montana," he said, "but he didn't recognize me, Doc. He had been trying all day to catch up with me. He wanted to give me that envelope. He was dying when he asked me to see that Arrant Canady got it."

Mays slipped the certified copy of Laura Canady's marriage license out and read it. He looked at Slade. "Arrant Canady should have lived long enough to see this," he said harshly.

Slade shrugged. "She's Philip's wife all right," he said evenly. "But I want you to do one thing for me, Doc. Don't tell her about this. Don't tell anyone. Put that envelope away in some safe place and write out a note for me, authorizing me to take over at Starlight —"

Mays considered this through the pain over his eyes. "You're taking over a lot of trouble," he said slowly. "You'll be bucking Crescent, a tough outfit. Judge Selman's been eyeing Starlight for a year. With no apparent heirs to Canady's spread, he's been getting ready to move in. He's been playing a legal game up to now — but he won't take your move without kicking up a fuss."

"I've met Judge Selman — and Crescent," Slade said shortly.

Mays smiled, a sad drooping of his lips. "Where have I been these past few days?" he murmured. It was a rhetorical question, aimed at himself. He felt adrift again, since Arrant Canady's death, and Badwater no longer meant anything to him. It was just a place where he had stopped for a little while in his aimless wandering.

He went around his desk and sat down, found paper in a drawer and used a quill pen. His hand was unsteady, but he took care to make the note readable. He folded it and handed it to Slade.

"Starlight's yours. I'll keep that marriage copy for Laura in my desk, locked up. But I'm telling you now, Slade, I intend that Laura Canady

60

shall have her share of the spread. Hobbs believed her, and I did, too. Hobbs believed in her enough to get killed for her." He made a wry face. "I'm afraid I'll keep my feelings sentimental. I'm not a man for trouble, Slade."

"Half of Starlight will be hers," Slade promised.

Mays eyed the bitter, cold-eyed man, trying to fathom what lay behind his words.

"Canady didn't talk much about you, Slade, but he had you on his conscience. What did he owe you?"

Slade's smile was as bleak as winter ice. "His life," he said, and went out, his limp barely noticeable.

Chapter Six

Slade rode out of Badwater on a pinto he had hired at the livery stable. The flat winter sun broke through a break in the overcast, spilling a sickly glow over the land. It did nothing to relieve the chill in the air.

He followed the road south of town, keeping his eyes alerted for sign of his big roan. A mile past the last building, the big shod hoof marks of the stallion dipped into an arroyo that angled upward to a low, brush-covered ridge.

Slade turned off the road and followed the arroyo to the ridge. The roan's trail was easy to follow. Five minutes later he pulled the pinto to a halt in a brush-enclosed wash.

A cayuse snorted from alder thickets on the slope. Slade grinned. He waited until the horse appeared, plunging down-slope, stirrups flapping loosely. The big stud came alongside, snorting suspiciously at the wary pinto. Slade rubbed his palm over the roan's nose, his eyes narrowing at the five-inch scratch between the animal's eyes. It looked as if a gun butt had been the cause of it.

"Had trouble, eh?" he said softly.

The roan snorted. Slade slipped into the animal's saddle. Leaning over, he looped the pinto's reins around the saddle horn and gave the animal a slap on the rump. The pinto turned back, heading for town.

Slade rode back to the road and swung south. A mile distant, the land fell away in a gradual slope. From the height it was like looking into a vast, irregular bowl. A wall of gray rock, sparsely timbered and known locally as the Breakers, curved along the western lip of the Basin. Low ragged hills hemmed in the valley on the north and west, fading into the bleak, inhospitable scarps of *Los Perdidos*.

Big Timber Creek glinted like tarnished silver in the sullen afternoon light, following along the base of the Breakers. Up where the ridge planed down to a low gentle pass was Siding, whistle stop on the T & P spur, hidden behind a knoll of earth.

Cutting off from the main stream, Little Timber sliced across the Basin in a series of slow, placid loops. In the center of the Basin, tucked within one of Little Timbers wide loops, Arrant Canady had built Starlight.

Starlight was a big sprawling place — a man's ranch. The main house was scarcely distinguishable from the bunkhouse — both were squat and utilitarian buildings. A cold wind raised dust across the yard, fluttering old, yellowed sheets of paper before it. A pile of tin cans in various stages of rust were heaped alongside a low shack from which wood smoke curled from the stone chimney.

Slade paused to take a long look at the place.

He compared Starlight and Pitchfork, set among low, rolling Montana hills. It was not as big as Starlight, but Canady had built the place for his wife, and it still retained a clean, homey look when Slade had joined Pitchfork.

Arrant was a widower of two years, with a young, spoiled boy on his hands and little ambition. Slade had taken charge, sunk into Pitchfork the savings he had managed to accumulate since the war, and put a lot of energy behind it. Pitchfork grew and made money . . . and lost it through the careless, insolent fingers of young Philip Canady.

Some men, wanting their sons to follow in their footsteps, are hard on their children. Arrant was not one of them. He had closed his eyes to Philip's faults and waited for the boy to grow up. He had backed Philip in every argument Slade had with him, and even now, in death, he had not let go of the hope that his son would come home and take over what he had left behind.

Slade pulled his thoughts from Montana. A loud argument was going on in the cook shack. It was loud enough to bring a slender, good-looking puncher to the door of the bunkhouse. The man stared at Slade with a hostile expression, but he voiced no greeting or objection to Slade's presence.

The galley door banged violently open. A long, stringy man with a sad old face and stained steerhorn mustache came out, carrying a battered leather grip in his fist.

He looked up, saw Slade, and a challenging sneer twisted his angry face. "You can go to blazes, too!" he said, and turned away, heading for the barn.

Slade grinned.

A tall, dark-haired man in his middle thirties came to the galley door and looked after the hurrying man with the suitcase. He had a worried expression.

"Jeb!" he called. "Damn it, I'm still boss here!"

He saw Slade watching him, and he stiffened, licked his lips. His shoulders sagged.

Two men pushed up behind him, crowding him down the three wooden steps. One was a heavy-shouldered man with a square red face and close-cropped, sandy hair. The other, thin and consumptive-looking and dark as an Indian, had a crooked Mexican cheroot in a corner of his mouth. Both men packed hardware.

The blocky man said: "Aw, let the sorehead go, Arch. His cooking stunk, anyhow!"

The tall man bit his lips. He looked at Slade with unfriendly eyes. "What do you want, feller?"

Slade said: "You Arch Nelson?"

The young man nodded.

Slade took the note Doc Mays had written out for him and handed it to the frowning Starlight man.

Nelson read it once and glanced up sharply, his lips thinning hard against his teeth. Then he read it again.

The blocky man standing behind him growled: "What's this joker want, Arch?"

Arch Nelson glanced at Slade. Slade's cold glance rested on the scowling man behind Arch. "You work for Starlight?" His question was curt.

The blocky man sneered. "I don't reckon that's any of yore business, fella!"

Arch Nelson made an attempt at pacification. "This is Al Cramer, Mr. Slade. The man on the steps is Lee Whitehead. They work for Crescent, a spread west of here." He looked at Slade, no expression on his face. "They've been giving Starlight a hand."

His voice had a flat stiffness that told Slade the statement was a lie. The two Crescent men were too arrogantly sure of themselves. A couple of gun-fast gents, Slade thought grimly, that Judge Selman had ordered onto Starlight after Arrant Canady's death as an advance force.

Slade eased out of saddle. Down by the barn the cook who had quit had turned around and was looking back at them. Several other men had joined the good-looking puncher in the bunkhouse doorway.

Slade's tone was short. "We can do without Crescent help, Nelson. See that they saddle up and ride." He started past Cramer toward the galley steps.

The Crescent man thrust a thick, hairy arm

across Slade's path. "Just a minute, big fella!" he growled. "Who gave you any authority around here?"

Slade stopped. He indicated the note in Nelson's hand. "I'm running Starlight now," he said quietly. "Dr. Mays' orders."

Cramer looked at Nelson, who grinned and handed him the note. Whitehead leaned against the door frame. "Put the big jasper straight, Al. Tell him who's really running Starlight!"

Cramer snatched the note from Nelson's fingers, read it slowly, then crumpled it in his fist.

"The doc's got a sense of humor," he rasped. "So have I." His grin was a wicked sneer. "I'm so funny I'm gonna make you eat this, fella."

Slade's eyes went a muddy gray. Lee Whitehead was still relaxed against the door, confident of Cramer's ability to handle what he seemed intent on starting.

"I wouldn't try to be too funny," Slade warned harshly.

Al Cramer laughed. He shot out a thick arm, reaching for Slade's coat front. He didn't see Slade move. Slade's open palm slapped his arm aside. Steel fingers dug into his shoulder, bringing a grunt to his lips. He was whirled around before he could gain his balance, and Slade's forearm slid across his throat, cutting off his wind. Cramer's heels dragged in the dirt as Slade stepped back several paces.

For a whisker of a moment Whitehead was

caught off guard, digested the unexpected turn of events. Then he reached for his Colt.

Slade's .45 scorched Cramer's pants with its muzzle blast. The sallow Crescent gunslinger jerked and fell back against the galley door, his gun arm shattered above the elbow. His cheroot hung limply from his lips, then fell, trailing ash and sparks.

Cramer was choking. His eyes bulged in his head.

Slade eased the pressure of his arm. "Tch, tch," he said, shaking his head. "Maybe you've not been getting enough to eat lately."

He reached for the crumpled letter in Cramer's fist. Chuckling, he began stuffing it between the Crescent gunman's parted lips.

Cramer gagged. Slade let him go. The blocky man's knees gave and he went down on them. Rage distorted his reason. He reached for his holstered Colt.

His eyes seemed to come together in his head as they focused on the muzzle held within an inch of his nose. A sickly pallor spread across his face.

"Eat it!" Slade snapped.

Cramer ate it. He had a time getting the note down past his bruised throat. When he had gulped the last particle down, Slade said: "These jaspers have mounts, Arch?"

Nelson nodded dumbly. He had just witnessed an event he had not believed possible. Crescent gunmen had run the Basin so long he couldn't believe what he had just seen.

"Get them!"

Nelson turned and sprinted for the barn.

Fifteen minutes later Cramer climbed into saddle. Whitehead had been helped into his. He sagged over his saddle horn, biting his lips against the pain of his broken arm. His eyes tried to find Slade, but they were watery with pain.

Slade said flatly: "Tell the judge that Starlight won't be needing Crescent help from now on, Cramer."

The blocky man nodded. His eyes were dark with rage and humiliation, but he didn't trust his voice.

They rode out of the yard. They were specks on the cold gray road to town when Slade turned on Nelson. His voice was blunt.

"Get cookie back. Get the rest of the boys into the galley. I'm taking over Starlight, and I'm starting now!"

Nelson managed a weak protest. "I'll wait until Ben Hobbs gets back —"

"Then you'll wait until hell freezes over!" Slade snapped. "Ben is dead! I'm giving you a choice. You can quit and ride out of here right now, or you can stay and listen to what I have to say. What'll it be, Arch?"

Arch bit his lips. "I'll hang around a bit, Mr. Slade. I promised Arrant Canady I'd stay. . . ."

Chapter Seven

Counting Arch Nelson and the cook who had been persuaded to return, there were six men left of the original outfit. They gathered around the long wooden table in the galley to listen to the new boss of Starlight.

Slade wasted no words.

"I'm Gilbert Slade," he said. "I knew Arrant Canady back in Montana. He owed me something; something more than he could ever pay."

Slade stood by the stove, a rangy man with a bleak, bitter smile. "That's why he left half of Starlight to me. I don't know about his son, Philip. Maybe he's dead. And I don't know about that woman in Badwater who claims to be Philip's wife. Maybe she has a right to half of Starlight." He paused and looked them over — six undecided men facing a future that could only hold trouble.

"I'll repeat it, boys — I don't know about Philip or his widow. But I'm here. And I'm going to run Starlight. I'm going to hold this spread against Judge Selman. I intend to make it what Arrant Canady tried to. To do it I'm going to need men willing to work — and maybe to fight. I don't intend to hire gunslingers — I'm not going to pay gunfighter wages. But I have a proposition for you. I don't know what Arrant Canady left besides this ranch. Not much in hard cash, I understand."

The men shifted, glanced at one another.

"I don't have any money, either," Slade said flatly. "Maybe I won't be able to pay wages for a few months — just keep. And if we go under, that's all you will have had —"

"It ain't only money," Arch cut in, "that keeps a hand working. Mr. Canady treated us right. Starlight was a good ranch to work for."

Slade nodded. "I'll keep it that way. And if we beat Crescent, there'll be something more than wages in it for those of you who stick. But that's the way things stand now. Ben Hobbs is dead. I'll be running Starlight on a shoestring — and I don't have to tell you the kind of trouble we're facing. I ran into a sample of it in town."

Arch walked over to the galley stove, shook the coffee pot, heard it slosh, and poured some into a mug. He turned and faced Slade.

"What happened to Ben?"

Slade told them what had happened in the Murado House, and threw in with no flourishes his run-in with Selman's court in Badwater.

Arch wore a worried scowl. "Judge Selman's been after Starlight from the day he came to the Basin," he volunteered. "He tried to buy into a partnership, but old Canady caught onto him, I reckon. The old man was pretty sour on things his last year anyway. He knew he didn't have much longer to live. He kept trying to get his boy to come back. Advertised in papers all over the country. Then this girl showed up in Badwater, claiming to be his daughter-in-law. She rode over to the ranch with Matt Kingston. She told Canady she had brought her marriage license with her, but someone stole it the first night she was in town."

"Canady didn't believe her?"

Nelson shook his head. "Ben Hobbs believed her. He an' the old man had quite an argument that night." Nelson grinned. "Hobbs claimed Arrant must have gone blind as a bat not to see the resemblance between the button and Philip Canady. Hobbs probably knew what he was talking about — none of us here ever saw Canady's son. But Arrant was plumb set in his thinking. He wanted more than this woman's say-so. Finally Ben ups an' swears he'll ride clear to Arizona to get it for him."

Slade stood by the head of the plank table, his right foot raised and resting on the bench. He felt the old twinge of pain in his lower back, and it brought the long pain-wracked months into focus. And then he looked beyond this, to Ben Hobbs riding as segundo for Pitchfork — a lanky, leathery man who lived his job. Ben had looked old and indestructible when Slade had first come to Pitchfork — he still looked the same the afternoon he had died at the Murado House.

But Philip Canady . . . ? The old impatience rose like bile in Slade when he thought of

Canady's son: a boy who had never done a decent thing in his life; who was born running . . . from responsibility, from honor, from himself.

But he had married the woman now in Badwater, and it was his son he had met this morning. Starlight was his, left to him in lieu of a greater debt . . . but half of this spread belonged to this woman who had made the great mistake of believing in Philip Canady.

He took a slow deep breath.

"Ben's dead," he reminded curtly. "I'm running Starlight. And it's time we got down to business. How many cows are wearing Starlight's iron?"

"Last tally we marked sixty-eight hundred on the books," Nelson muttered. He was still undecided; a young man who balked at hard-handed authority. "That was a year ago, Mr. Slade. Since then we've had trouble with Crescent."

He looked across the table at the good-looking puncher Slade had spotted standing in the bunkhouse doorway when he had first ridden into Starlight.

"What's yore guess, Hal?"

Hal Taylor shrugged. There was a sullen expression in his blue eyes. "We lost three good men who were patrolling the broken country east of the *Canyoncitos,*" he said "I know we've been losing beef there. But we didn't have the kind of guns to buck Crescent then. And we haven't had a roundup since fall a year ago —"

"Ben wanted to send for some of the old Pitch-fork hands," Nelson put in. "Claimed they could run Crescent out of the Basin." The smile on his hard face doubted this. "But Mr. Canady couldn't see it. He didn't seem to want to talk about the old Montana spread."

"How many hands worked for Starlight?" Slade asked.

"Twelve — a year ago. Then Crescent started crowding us. After we lost Walt, Eddie an' Radek, some of the others quit. Ben tried to hire men in Badwater, but Crescent blocked him. Mr. Canady no longer cared. He'd sit out on the porch and watch the road and listen to Ben and not make a move. He kept telling Ben, 'He'll come. I know he will.' " Nelson made an abrupt gesture. "I reckon he was waiting for his son to show up."

"Could be," Slade said. But he was thinking of what Dr. Mays had told him, and he knew Arrant had been expecting him. Which meant that Canady had known all along that he was alive — must have known during the grim year he had lain in that old sheepherder's shack that he was alive, and had let him be.

"Most of the old hands quit," Nelson went on. "We kinda hung on —"

"Speak for yoreself, Arch," Hal cut in coldly. "I was ready to cut my string. I stayed this long because I had promised Ben to wait until he got back." There was bitter defiance in his voice. "I

74

still haven't made up my mind to stay, Mr. Slade. It's going to take more than talk to beat Crescent. And none of us here, barring you, are much good with a Colt."

Slade looked out the window. The ground was frozen and the wind had a cutting edge; it made a thin, wailing sound in the chimney.

Arrant Canady had left him Starlight. But the old man had left him a pile of trouble, too.

"I'll take care of that end," he said. His voice was flat and cold.

Arch started to sneer. Then he looked at Hal and shrugged.

"I'll stay," he announced. "But we're gonna need help. And we're gonna need supplies —"

Slade looked at the others. Hal was still undecided. But the other two, George Masel and Billy Stodel, went along with Arch. They were about Arch's age, and had a lot in common.

Starlight's cook was already fussing with the stove; he turned and eyed Slade with the frank belligerency of an old hand. "I'll have dinner on the table in an hour, if one of these loafers will quit beefing and rustle in more firewood."

Slade nodded. He started for the door, but stopped at Hal's question.

"What about Crescent?"

Slade looked at him. "You own a rifle?"

Hal nodded. "And a Colt."

"Wear them. Stay out of town for the time being. Ride in pairs when you ride on Starlight business. Keep wide of Crescent." He paused a moment, and slowly let his eyes rest on each man there.

"If you're pushed — use your own judgment."

He went out, closing the door behind him. Arch moved to the window, and the others crowded around him. They watched Slade lead his cayuse toward the barn, noticed the slight limp.

Arch looked at Hal. "I'll take care of that end," he mimicked harshly. "*Mister* Slade, you talk big. I reckon I'll stick around — just to see how big that talk is!"

"I saw him handle Cramer and Whitehead," the cook snapped. He was standing back from the window, an old man disgusted at the wait-and-see attitude of the younger hands. "That's enough for me." He spat into the woodbox behind the stove. "I'm saying Starlight's got itself a real boss this time!"

Arch grinned. "Amen," he said thinly.

Matt Kingston felt low. He came out of the Trail Saloon and paused on the sagging porch, eyeing the ramshackle buildings of Badwater. The three drinks he had taken made no impression on him; he felt no glow, no warming protection against the rawness out here in the street.

He had let Laura off early to look after Tommy, and put the finishing touches to tomorrow's edition of the *Gazette* himself. He had rewritten the lead story himself, going over it three times, and he was still unsatisfied.

He should have been elated. He had waited for almost a year to have a story like this one he was running under a banner head: JUDGE SELMAN'S KANGAROO COURT BACKFIRES.

But what had happened to Selman and his bunch of outlaws was offset by the death of Ben Hobbs, and by the lack of evidence that Laura Canady had ever been married to Arrant Canady's son, Philip.

He had hurried over to Josel's Funeral Parlors and found that Josel had already gone through Ben's clothes and laid his personal belongings aside in a little box. There was no envelope there; nothing to show that Ben had ever gotten as far as Bisbee. And he had not suspected Josel — the man was honest beyond a doubt.

It left three possibilities. Either Ben had never reached Bisbee, or Gil Slade was lying. He tried not to think of the other possibility: that Laura might have lied too. But it nagged at him anyway, and he flushed at his seeming disloyalty.

He saw the stage coming down the slope, and his gaze lifted above it to the darkening sky over the Breakers. He had lived here long enough to know the suddenness of these winter blizzards — the sharp, icy winds that of a sudden spit biting sleet. Hunching up his collar, he headed for the hotel where he lived.

The stage drew up before the door as he came up the walk. Two passengers came out. One was the portly wife of Tom Laird, who ran the hardware store in the next block. Matt knew she had gone to San Antonio to visit an aunt and to do some shopping. Laura had written the story herself.

The other passenger was a well-dressed, blond man as tall as Matt. A small yellow mustache made a thin line under a thin hooked nose. A heavy gold watch chain looped across the fifth button of a fawn-colored vest caught the cold light of day and focussed attention on it.

He was a handsome man, and for a city man, Matt thought idly, he looked fit and hard.

The driver handed a light brown pigskin bag down to the passenger, and Matt saw him press a bill into the driver's rough palm. The driver said: "Thank you, Mr. Canady." He swung back up into the seat and clucked to his team.

Matt stopped. The name penetrated slowly, like molasses running down the sides of a jar. *Canady!*

The blond man picked up Mrs. Laird's heavy suitcase. He had a charming manner, a nice smile. The woman appeared flustered. She brushed at straggling wisps of hair under her feather-trimmed hat, although she was almost old enough to be the man's mother.

"Mr. Canady — you are a gentleman!" She turned as Tom Laird himself came up the walk. "Tom — this is Philip Canady. Arrant Canady's boy!"

Tom was a short, heavy man with a dull face. He nodded awkwardly, picked up his wife's bag.

"You got here a little late," he said. "I've been waiting since ten this morning."

He turned away, pulling his startled wife with him.

The blond man looked after them, a thin, supercilious smile under his mustache.

Matt roused himself. "Philip Canady?"

"Right." The newcomer turned and looked at Matt. He gestured after Tom Laird. "Awkward fellow, wasn't he?"

Matt ignored the irrelevant remark. His heart was pounding heavily. This man was Laura's husband! Deep inside him he had acknowledged this possibility — and dreaded it!

"Are you Arrant Canady's son?"

The man's slate gray eyes hardened. "Well," he answered slowly, "I am, if he hasn't disowned me." He chuckled. "I haven't seen the old man since I left home. Up in Montana, that was. The old Pitchfork Ranch." He pulled a clipping out of his wallet, held it out to Matt. "Ran across this ad in a New Orleans paper about three weeks ago, asking for me to come home. So I softened up and — Hey!" he said sharply. "Something wrong?"

Matt nodded, tight-lipped. "You softened up a little late, Mr. Canady! Your father died six days ago."

Philip Canady looked past Matt. He didn't say anything for a moment, but Matt couldn't see any change in the man's hard face. After a while Philip said: "Tough." That was his only comment.

What the devil! Matt thought angrily. *The man hasn't seen Arrant Canady in years! But still, the old man had been his father!*

"Seems like I made the trip out to this uncivilized neck of Texas for nothing," Philip commented. He glanced down the wind-swept, dirty street and shuddered slightly. "Well, I can always leave on the next stage going back East."

"Your wife's here," Matt said. His breath felt hot in his throat.

The man started. "Wife?"

Matt nodded. "She's living at Ma Crane's with little Tommy."

Canady's eyes narrowed. "I don't know what you're trying to pull on me, mister," he said coldly. "But I haven't got a wife or a kid." He bent to pick up his bag, sniffed audibly, and his smile was icy as he straightened. "No wonder," he snapped. "You're drunk!"

Matt's fists balled. "Why you — !"

The man dropped his bag. His left hand dipped inside his coat and emerged with a short-barreled .38 pistol. "I wouldn't get tough about it," he warned harshly. "You might get hurt."

Matt didn't move. Philip Canady laughed shortly, contemptuously. He picked up his bag and went into the hotel without a backward glance. Matt looked after him. The warmth had gone out of the pit of his stomach. After a while he turned and went back to the Trail Saloon.

The bartender grinned as he poured his drink.

"Hitting it up tonight, eh? This one's three past your limit, Matt. What are you celebrating?"

"The prodigal son's return!" Matt snarled.

The barman retreated, muttering.

The newspaperman drank his whiskey without feeling it, hardly conscious of the act. He was trying to find the meaning of Philip Canady's denial. Had Laura lied to him — to Ben Hobbs — to Arrant Canady? Was she just a scheming woman who had seen a chance to inherit one of the biggest cattle ranches in the county?

Yet, he thought miserably, Hobbs had believed in her. The Starlight ramrod had died trying to prove Laura was Arrant Canady's daughter-in-law — that her son was Arrant's grandchild!

He shook his head, dispelling his doubts, feeling a sort of guiltiness that he had entertained them. More likely Philip Canady didn't want to own up to having a wife — that would be more understandable in the light of his desertion. But Laura would prove him a liar. The man couldn't deny her, once she confronted him in person!

The thought of what that might lead to made him miserable. She was Philip's lawfully wedded wife. In the interests of young Tommy, a reconciliation was possible. Matt was breathing harshly as he tossed money on the bar and left. . . .

Laura came into Ma Crane's kitchen, greeting him with a smile. Ma Crane discreetly left the room, taking Tommy with her.

"Matt! You've been celebrating!" There was no displeasure, only surprise. She stood off, still smiling, as though she had never seen him like this, and somehow found him more human because of it.

He looked at her, not finding ready words at the moment. They had worked together for eleven months. He knew her every gesture, the little frown over her eyes when she concentrated on some bit of composition, the small dimple in her left cheek. He had worked with her and fallen in love with her, and yet he had felt the barrier of age and it had created a stiffness in him — he felt awkward and kept silent in her presence.

Her smile faded slowly. "Matt! What is it?"

His voice blurted out, half angry, half condemning. "Your husband's in town, Laura! Philip Canady arrived on the Rawlins stage ten minutes ago!"

He saw the shock of it go through her, almost as if he had walked up and slapped her face. The warmth died out of her eyes.

"Philip!"

Matt nodded. "He's registered at the Stage Hotel." He hesitated, then went on brutally, "A handsome devil, Laura. But he disclaimed ever having a wife!"

Laura's chin lifted. "Matt — I'm going to see him. I want him to tell me that — to my face!"

Kingston waited while Laura got her coat.

They went out together, down the darkening street. There was the smell of snow in the icy wind. Matt's gaze flicked toward the south trail; he half expected to see Gil Slade show up.

He had nosed around after his encounter with the cold-eyed man who had successfully bucked Judge Selman's Badwater court and found out from Dr. Mays that he was the Gilbert Slade to whom Arrant Canady had left half of Starlight. But Dr. Mays had clammed up after that, and Matt got nothing more from him.

He and Laura went into the hotel. A bored whiskey salesman occupied one of the lobby chairs, reading an old edition of the *Gazette*. The desk clerk was playing a game of solitaire on the counter beside the register.

Matt said: "We'd like to see Mr. Philip Canady. He registered a half-hour ago."

The clerk smirked at Laura, then went dead-pan at the quick scowl on Matt's face. He yelled for a colored boy, who came shuffling out of the kitchen and went upstairs.

Matt waited with grim impatience. He watched Laura's face. Her chin was up, and he recognized the twin red spots on her cheeks. He didn't want to be there, yet he felt he shouldn't leave her. . . .

Philip Canady came down the wide stairs. He had washed and shaved and put on a fresh white shirt. His hair was combed back and his smile was pleasant. He saw Laura and Matt and stopped, a frown displacing his easy smile.

Matt faced him. "Gun or no gun, mister," he warned tensely, "if you deny this woman is your wife, I'll break your neck! So help me!"

Laura's sharp voice cut him off and left him fumbling.

"Matt! This man isn't Philip Canady! He's not my husband!"

The clerk's head jerked up. The whiskey drummer dropped his paper and twisted in his chair.

The blond man looked from Laura's blazing eyes to Matt's slack face. "What is this?" he demanded harshly. "Some sort of blackmail?"

Matt looked at Laura. There was a wordless appeal in his stunned face.

Laura's voice was scornful. "This man is not Philip Canady, Matt!"

The blond man took a forward step. "I don't know what your game is, *lady* —" He stressed the word, sneering, and Matt moved violently, swinging for Canady's face. Philip staggered back against the newel post of the lobby stairs. Matt moved in after him.

The .38 made a flat crack in the hotel.

Matt stopped. He looked down at the hole in his left shoulder, as if he couldn't believe it had happened.

Laura darted in front of him, ignoring the gun in the blond man's hand. "Matt —" Her voice broke. "Matt — come away! He'll kill you!"

Matt tried to push her aside. Then nausea hit him in the stomach, and his legs went rubbery.

Laura knelt beside him, her face white. The shot had attracted a small group of curious townspeople by the time someone summoned the marshal.

Bill Talley had a bandage under his hat. He took in the scene without comment and listened silently as the blond man explained.

"I'm Philip Canady. I arrived on the Rawlins stage an hour ago. This man met me when I got off the stage and accused me of having a wife and boy!" He looked down at Laura, who was still kneeling beside Matt's unconscious form. "I've no idea what it's all about, Sheriff." Talley made no comment at this error in his title. "When I told him I never saw the woman before, he jumped me!"

Talley's smile was crooked. "Too bad you didn't kill him!" he commented callously.

Laura turned, her fists clenching. But Matt's plight sapped her anger, brought tears to her eyes. "Please," she begged, "someone get Dr. Mays. And help me get him to his room. Please."

One man nodded and went out. Several others, avoiding the marshal's scowling stare, picked up Kingston and carried him upstairs to his room. Laura followed them.

The marshal looked at the blond man. "You say yo're Philip Canady? Old Arrant Canady's boy?"

"I didn't come to Badwater prepared to prove it," the other said defiantly. "I expected to find my father alive. Ben Hobbs will know me —"

"Hobbs is dead, too," the marshal said grimly.

Canady said: "Oh!" He looked around at the faces watching him. "I haven't much with me, Sheriff," he apologized. "A couple of letters from my father that I never answered. One from a friend. And here's a letter of reference from my employer in New Orleans."

Marshal Talley examined the letters.

Canady was tugging at his ring. It was a heavy gold band topped by a red stone. "Mother gave this to me on my sixteenth birthday," he said, handing it to the lawman.

Talley read the inscription aloud: "To my son, Philip Canady, May 17, 1884."

The marshal nodded. "That's proof enough for me, Mr. Canady." He turned his glance to the stairs up which Laura had disappeared.

"I always knew she was a phoney!"

Chapter Eight

An icy wind, riding point for the storm gathering itself north of the Breakers, had scattered a light mantle of snow across the frozen land during the night.

Slade opened the galley door and looked up at the slate gray morning sky. Behind him Jeb was fussing over breakfast, and the warmth of the cook stove steamed the galley windows. The smell of newly brewed coffee made a pleasant aroma in the galley.

Arch Nelson came to the door of the bunkhouse across the frozen yard. The puncher glanced up at the lowering sky, blew on his hands, and made a quick run for the warmth of the cook shack. Slade stepped aside to let him inside.

"Looks like more snow," Arch grumbled. He stood with his back to the stove until Jeb, arriving with a bowl of fresh buckwheat batter, shooed him away. He found a mug and poured coffee from the pot on the stove.

"Been here three years, and every winter's different," he complained. "Might get a blizzard tomorrow, and a mild spell next week."

Slade finished his coffee and placed the empty cup on the long wooden table. He closed the door and reached for his Bull Durham, and Arch ran the palm of his hand across the harsh stubble on his jaw.

"There's a lot of work to be done, if you want still to have a spread come spring," Arch said.

Slade nodded. "We'll hold off the tally until the weather breaks," he decided. "I'll want to take a look around, find out how much feed we'll need, look over our fence —"

"We've got two trouble spots," Arch put in: "our western line fence where it meets Crescent range; and the country north of the Breakers. We get a drift into those canyons every bad storm and stand to lose a high percentage if we don't get them out before a heavy snow seals them in."

Slade shrugged. He had fought winter storms before, on Pitchfork — and he knew what a blizzard and bad freeze could do to range cattle. He knew, too, that it would take money, feed and men to bring sixty-eight hundred head of cattle through even a normal winter with only moderate losses. And he had not yet seen enough of Starlight to be able to judge its weak points.

He saw Arch watching him, and he knew that the young puncher still reserved judgment. Arch had worked for Arrant Canady and for Ben Hobbs; he resented having a stranger walk in and take over Starlight.

But Slade understood the man. And he knew he would be on trial here before this remnant of Starlight's crew.

It irritated and annoyed him. Canady's death

had taken all the steam from him. He had come to Starlight Basin to kill a man, only to find him already dead — and to find himself saddled with Starlight's troubles.

Slade thought of the woman in Badwater who was young Philip Canady's wife. He had a moment's ironic wonder at what any woman could have seen in Arrant Canady's spoiled boy. Enough to marry him, obviously. But she had probably been too young for mature appraisal, and Philip Canady could be likable when he wanted.

Anyway, it didn't concern him. But, he thought with dry amusement, Philip's wife was his partner, whether he liked it or not.

Arch said with that slow undercurrent of cool hostility: "We'll still need more help, Mr. Slade."

Slade looked at him. Arch flushed under his direct stare, but didn't drop his gaze.

"I'm riding into town this morning to hire more help," Slade said coldly.

Arch's smile bordered dangerously on a sneer. "I don't want to discourage you, Mr. Slade. But Mr. Canady couldn't hire anyone in Badwater —"

"I'm not Arrant Canady!" Slade snapped.

Arch's lips tightened, and Slade knew that this show of anger had not helped with this man.

"Better wait until the rest of the boys are up," he suggested. "We'll ride with you —"

"You'll stay here," Slade cut in. "I'll want to

know how much feed we've got on hand, what condition the wagons are in. I'll want a complete report of what we have, barring the beef tally."

Arch nodded, his eyes sullen. But he had one more say. "Crescent runs Badwater, Mr. Slade. The judge won't take losing Starlight easy."

Slade's smile was brief and wintery. "There's nothing he can do about it now." He pinched out his cigaret, dropped it into the brass spittoon by the stove.

"Way I see it, Selman had planned to take over a spread that had no heirs. When Arrant Canady died, Starlight was left wide open for anyone to take over; anyone with guns to make it stick. That's why he sent two men after Ben to make sure Hobbs wouldn't get back with any evidence that might prove that the woman waiting in Badwater was legally entitled to Starlight."

"I know why Judge Selman waited," Arch said. "But you're underrating him, if you figure he's played his last hand."

The door opened again and Hal Taylor came inside. He had a telegram in his hands which he handed Slade.

"This came in the day after we buried Arrant Canady," he said. "Arch was away, so I stuck it in my locker and forgot about it until this morning."

Slade read the message addressed to Arrant Canady:

Arriving at Siding the 25th.
Have someone meet me. Bless you. Martha.

Slade stared at the wire, his mind reaching back to a plump motherly woman who had taken care of the household chores at Pitchfork.

"Martha," he muttered.

"Arrant's old housekeeper," Arch put in. "The 25th? Jumping Jehoshaphat! That's Thursday!" He looked at Slade. "What we gonna do with the woman now?"

"Why is she coming down here anyway?" Slade muttered.

"She was asked," Nelson said. He made a gesture. "The Old Man was getting pretty sour these last months. After his last attack, Doc Mays warned him he'd have to keep out of the saddle — take things real easy. It was Ben who suggested Mr. Canady should wire his old housekeeper to come down and take care of him."

Taylor made a wry face. "Well, she'll only be in the way here now."

"I'll ride to Siding to meet her, when she arrives," Slade settled the matter. "Maybe I can get her to go back on the next train."

Taylor poured himself a cup of coffee and walked with it to the steamy window as Slade went out. He wiped the pane and stared into the snow-whitened yard, letting his coffee cool. Arch was still standing by the stove, the sneer lingering on his lips.

Jeb came up behind Taylor.

"Ate two stacks of buckwheat cakes an' drank four cups of coffee," he said proudly, watching Slade head for the barn where he had stabled his cayuse. "Now there's a man I kin cotton to, Hal."

Taylor ignored him. He was thinking how he had liked working for Starlight, before Selman bought out the small spread that was Crescent and stocked it with gunmen.

He watched Slade come out of the barn, leading his saddled roan, swing aboard and ride out of the yard without looking back. There was something obdurate in that figure outlined against the ominous sky; it gave Taylor a sense of unyielding solidity as enduring as the ragged, eternal Breakers.

"You know, Arch," Taylor said impulsively, turning to Nelson; "I've got a feeling he's big enough to do it."

"Do what?"

"Beat Crescent," Taylor replied.

Slade's roan ate up the miles to Badwater. It was close to noon when Slade pulled up before the *Gazette*'s closed doors. He found them locked, which surprised him. He had intended to see Matt Kingston about an ad in the *Gazette* concerning riders wanted for Starlight.

He thought Matt might have stepped out for an early dinner, but he remembered that today was the *Gazette*'s press day. He was looking up and down the street, frowning, when the barber next door said: "If you're looking for Matt Kingston, he won't be in today. He was shot last night. He's up in his room at the hotel."

Slade nodded his thanks, got back into saddle and rode to the hotel. He stopped by the desk long enough to find out from a smirking desk clerk in which room Matt was bedded down and went upstairs.

Dr. Mays was just coming out. He closed the door and looked at Slade, and Slade said: "How is he?"

Mays shrugged. "Good as can be expected. He'll be on his feet in a week, if he stays in bed."

Slade put his gaze on the closed door. "Maybe I'd better see him later, then."

Mays shrugged. "He's asleep. But you may as well go in, Mr. Slade. You might talk to your partner — Laura Canady." He avoided Slade's direct, questioning glance. "She'll tell you how it happened."

He moved past the frowning Slade, paused at the head of the stairs. "I'd like to see you before you leave town."

Slade watched him go down the stairs. There had been an air of mystery about Mays that irritated him. Matt Kingston had struck him as a man of uneven temper, and it had not particularly surprised him to learn Matt had been shot.

He knocked on the door. Laura Canady opened the door for him.

Slade had seen this woman yesterday; had had a brief glimpse of her when he had been marched past the *Gazette* by Marshal Talley. He looked at her now, judging her, and the appraisal was not flattering.

She looked tired. Her hair was undone, and her face was drawn, and there were sleepless circles under her eyes. She must have spent the night taking care of Kingston, he thought. She stared at him now with dull anxiety.

He said: "May I come in?"

She hesitated. "Mr. Kingston's just fallen asleep —"

"I won't disturb him." Slade pushed the door open and stepped inside and looked about the room. Kingston was an unmarried man, and his room had the spare, utilitarian look of a bachelor's room: a dresser, a chair, a small desk on which papers were scattered — a window opening on the main street. His bed was placed near the window.

Matt was lying on two pillows, his beard-shadowed face showing an unhealthy pallor against the white pillowcase.

Laura Canady pushed the door shut and leaned against it, made an ineffectual attempt to smooth her hair back.

"I'm Gilbert Slade," Slade said. "Dr. Mays must have told you about me. I've taken over at Starlight."

She nodded. Her face took on color as she walked into the room, motioned for him to take a chair. "I've heard."

He ignored the invitation to sit down. He was

94

studying this girl, or woman rather, trying to understand her. She was not what he had expected. She did not look like some ignorant back country girl who might easily have been taken in by Philip Canady's charm, or some hardened woman who may have learned of Philip's Pitchfork interests and married him for what she thought she could get out of the marriage.

"I came to town to see Matt," he said. "I hoped I might still be able to get a help wanted ad in this week's *Gazette*. I found Starlight short-handed —"

"There'll be no *Gazette* for some time, Mr. Slade," she interrupted. "Very possibly the *Gazette* may suspend publication entirely."

He shrugged. "I'm sorry to hear it." He looked at the sleeping figure. "Who did Matt get into trouble with?"

His question surprised her. "Don't you know? I thought Dr. Mays told you —"

"I met the doc in the hallway," Slade cut in. "He acted mighty queer about Matt being shot — but he preferred to let you tell me."

Her smile had a bitter tinge. "I'm afraid Dr. Mays has been somewhat confused by recent events, Mr. Slade. I don't think he was ever entirely convinced I am Philip Canady's wife. And after what happened yesterday, I'm afraid his doubts have increased considerably."

"He did act mysterious," Slade said. "But I have reason to believe he is quite sure you are

Mrs. Philip Canady."

She shook her head. "Yesterday afternoon a man arrived on the late stage. He said he was Philip Canady."

Slade started. But Laura didn't notice. She had turned to stare at the wall, her shoulders stiff, her voice thin and bitter.

"He was convincing enough to make Matt come looking for me. He seems to have convinced the law in Badwater that he is Philip Canady —"

"And you?" Slade's voice was flat.

"He's not Philip Canady! He's an impostor!"

Slade studied her stiff back, the way she held her head. Was she lying, trying to save face?

"How did Matt get hurt?"

She turned to face him. "Because Matt's in love with me. Because, despite his doubts, he wants to believe in me. We went to see this man — he is staying in the hotel — and when I saw him I knew he was not Philip Canady. I told him so, and Matt took exception to the remarks he made about me —"

On the bed Matt stirred, as though Laura's voice had reached through his clouded brain. He groaned and moved again, but his eyes remained closed and his breathing heavy.

Laura's voice dropped to a whisper, and the stiffness went out of her shoulders. "I don't care any more. If I had known the trouble my coming here would cause, I never would have come. Starlight isn't worth that to me — or to Tommy.

It was never worth the death of Ben Hobbs, or what's happened to Matt —"

"It's worth whatever you're willing to pay for it," Slade said. His voice was hard. "Arrant Canady owed me something he could never repay — alive. But he left half of Starlight to me when he died. The other half belongs to you and Tommy — or to Philip Canady, if he's still alive."

Her chin lifted. "I don't know if Philip is alive. I have never received a word from him from the day he walked out on me. But the man who's in town today, claiming to be Philip, is not the man I married."

Slade frowned. "Are you sure? A man can change —"

The woman's eyes met his. He saw they were gray with amber flecks. They had depth and integrity. She seemed to have come alive in the few minutes since she had opened the door for him. She stood straight and slim and the color in her face became her so that he was aware she was a beautiful woman still.

"It's been less than four years, Mr. Slade. A woman doesn't forget a man who's been her husband, no matter how much he might change." She flushed, shook her head. "Philip was tall and blond, yes. But he had a petulant mouth, a smile like a little boy's. There was a small scar over his left eye, shaped like a crescent — oh, there are a dozen ways a woman can know." Her eyes were steady on him. "This man is not Philip Canady, no matter what evidence he may have, or what Dr. Mays believes."

He was inclined to believe her. Anyway, he'd know if this stranger was Philip Canady when he saw him. Slade had had his run-ins with Arrant's boy too often not to have that weak, insolent, handsome face etched in his memory.

But he couldn't tell this woman he had known Philip. He was reluctant to reveal his connection with the Canadys. Now that Arrant Canady was dead, he felt a strange distaste for bringing up any of the bitter rancor of the past.

He could tell her about the certified proof of her marriage which was now entrusted to Mays. But any acknowledgment of her legal rights to a share in Starlight would only involve her in almost certain trouble with Crescent. For the moment it was best that only Mays know of that legal paper Ben Hobbs had been killed for.

"I believe you," he told her quietly. "But it would help if there were others in town who could identify the real Philip Canady."

She made a gesture of dismay. "Arrant Canady and Ben Hobbs appear to have been the only persons who knew Philip, other than myself. There might be someone in Montana who would remember. But that's eight hundred miles away —"

Slade remembered the telegram in his pocket. "I wouldn't give up hope," he said quietly. "If you're entitled to half of Starlight, Mrs. Canady, I'll see that you get it."

She faced him, moving up close so that he felt her nearness. "Why?" There was an honest directness about this woman. "Why should you bother? What difference does it make to you who inherits the other half of Starlight?"

"A great deal of difference," he said coldly. "I have never liked Philip Canady."

He turned and walked out while she stared after him, the import of his statement coming later, whitening her face. . . .

Chapter Nine

The wind wailed with icy cry along the deserted main street of Badwater. There was little inducement for men to be outdoors, and most of Badwater's inhabitants were glad to fortify themselves against the cold spell at any one of the half-dozen saloons that speckled the town's main business blocks.

Slade stepped out of the hotel lobby almost directly in Marshal Bill Talley's path. The big man was like a massive block of granite, crowding the walk. A dirty bandage showed under the rim of his hat.

He faced Slade, his weight shifting to his toes. His hands were jammed in the pockets of his short coat. He kept them there. But his small eyes glittered as they sized up the man in front of him. They were red and mean as a cornered grizzly's.

Slade prudently stepped back out of reach of Talley's big hands. He had felt the weight of this man's strength and did not intend to let the marshal use it on him again.

"Looking for me, Marshall?"

Talley licked his lips. "Not right now," he said. Caution tempered the hate in his eyes.

"Glad to hear it," Slade commented. His voice

was dry but his attitude was watchful. "I'm expecting to be around for a long time."

"So I heard." Talley sneered. "The new boss of Starlight."

"You questioning my legal rights to Canady's spread, Marshal?"

Talley shook his head. "That ain't my job. But I hear Arrant's boy, Philip Canady, is in town. Looks like you've got yoreself a partner."

"Could be," Slade murmured. "If he's Philip Canady —"

"He is!" Talley snarled. "His proof will stand up in any court. And mebbe you won't be in charge at Starlight long."

Slade shrugged. There was more behind the big marshal's talk than idle threat; the man was obviously holding something back.

"I'll worry about that when I come to it," he said coolly.

Talley's dark face congested. "A tough hombre, eh?" he ground out. "Real rough. Outgunned Teach. Put Lee Whitehead out of commission, an' made Cramer knuckle down to you —"

"Friends of yours?"

Talley's neck cords bulged at the easy insolence in Slade's tone. His voice thickened. "Real tough. Well, I like the tough ones. They cry louder when they break."

"I'm not crying," Slade murmured. He shifted slightly, a bleak grin on his lips.

"Some day —"

"Why not now?" Slade's voice pushed the lawman. He would have to face this man sooner or later, he realized. Talley was not the kind to forgive what had happened to him in the Open House.

But the big man didn't move.

Slade started forward. "You're in my way," he sneered.

Talley's head hunched forward; a murderous look muddied his eyes. But sanity caught up with him in time. He was no match for this coldly smiling man in a gunfight, and he knew it.

He stepped aside and moved on, his big shoulders thrusting against the bitter wind. . . .

Slade watched him until the marshal turned up a side street. Then he mounted and rode to Dr. Mays' office.

Mays had company: a tall, handsome blond man who was just getting ready to leave when Slade entered.

Dr. Mays looked flustered. "Gil — I'm glad you stopped in. I want you to meet Philip Canady. Arrant's boy," he added needlessly.

The blond man turned and measured Slade with a shrewd regard. He put out a hand. "Good to know you, Slade. Dr. Mays was just explaining to me about you." He smiled briefly. "It seems you and I are partners."

Slade nodded. "Looks that way." His voice was casual, holding no hint of what he felt.

Laura Canady was right. This was not Philip Canady. There was a surface resemblance, but not enough to fool anyone who had ever known Philip.

"Did you know my father?" The blond man's voice was politely curious.

"Some," Slade admitted.

"Must have been up in Montana," the other said. "You know — I don't remember you —" He shrugged. "But then, I was pretty wild in those days, Mr. Slade. Sort of felt I had my own life to lead. After Mother died I got out of hand —" He smiled apologetically. "I ran away from Pitchfork five years ago. Knocked around long enough to find that life isn't just one big picnic. I've been working in New Orleans these past two years."

It was a convincing speech. It was easy and natural, and Slade knew the man must have rehearsed it many times.

"I didn't know your father too well," Slade said. "I may have seen you at Pitchfork, though. You've changed some, I'd say."

A glitter passed briefly through the other's cold blue eyes. "Five years do things to a man," he murmured. Then he smiled. "I'm not kicking, mind you. But I'd like to know how it was that Dad left you half of Starlight, Mr. Slade."

Slade shrugged. "He owed me that much." He turned to Dr. Mays, who was sitting back in his chair, looking a bit uncomfortable. Mays had tidied up and pulled himself together since Slade had met him, but he still looked tired, and he had taken little pains with his morning shave.

"Arrant Canady was expecting me, wasn't he, Doc?"

Mays nodded. "That's why he asked me into the bank and had me and Frank Hobson witness his will. He said he had hoped to explain to you when you showed up, but now he thought he might not have time. He did say that Starlight was rightfully yours, Mr. Slade — at least a half-share was. And he wanted Frank and me to be sure you were told of this when you came."

The blond man waved his hand. "Oh, I'm not questioning Mr. Slade's right to Starlight," he said quickly. "Actually, I'm surprised Dad didn't cut me out entirely. He and I didn't get along too well, and after I left him I didn't even write —"

You're not Philip Canady, Slade thought, but you know a lot about him. You must have known Philip pretty well. But to get by with this, you have to know, with dead certainty, that the only two men in Starlight Basin who knew the real Philip Canady are dead!

The man posing as Arrant's son picked up his hat. "I'm really not a rancher, Mr. Slade. City life is more to my liking. So I'll not be staying long. In fact, I've about decided to leave on the stage tomorrow afternoon."

"Going back to New Orleans?"

The other nodded. "I've already received a good offer for my share of Starlight. I hope you don't mind, Mr. Slade, but I think I'll sell." He shook his head in an attempt at sorrow. "If my father was still alive, or Ben — But the way things are, the ranch here means nothing to me. Pitchfork was my home. I don't know a soul around here."

Slade nodded coldly. "I know how you feel, Mr. Canady. May I ask who you are selling to?"

"A Mr. Selman made me a good offer," the other replied. "A very generous offer. Of course," he smiled, "if you feel you can better it, I'd be glad to sell to you, Mr. Slade."

Slade grinned crookedly. "I'm afraid I couldn't match any offer of Mr. Selman's."

The man called Philip Canady seemed disappointed. "Well, I hope you have no hard feelings." He turned to Mays. "I'll be back in the morning, Doctor. You'll have the necessary papers ready then, I presume?"

Mays said: "I'll see Frank Hobson today."

"Just a minute, Mr. Canady," Slade said. Philip was at the door; he turned, frowning.

"I understand there's a woman in town with a small boy who claims to be your wife —"

The hard glitter came to stay in the blond man's eyes. "A preposterous attempt at blackmail!" he snapped. "I understand she has nothing to base her claims upon, other than her word —"

"And you?"

"I've satisfied Dr. Mays, and the local authorities, as to my identity, Mr. Slade." His eyes narrowed. "Why are you concerned with her?"

"Only insofar as I wouldn't want Starlight

involved in a legal wrangle after you leave," Slade said. "I'm sure you can understand my concern."

The other took a deep breath. "I understand. And I assure you that this woman has never been my wife. I've never seen her before yesterday, when she and that newspaper fellow tried to make trouble for me in the hotel."

Slade smiled. "I heard you're pretty handy with that under-arm pistol. Must be a rough town, this New Orleans —"

The blond man's eyes held a cool anger. "Quite."

"If you don't mind too much, Mr. Canady," Slade added smoothly, "I wish you'd hold off selling to Mr. Selman until after Thursday."

Canady stood by the door, a still, hard figure. "Why?"

"I'm willing to take the doc's word about your identity," Slade said. "But the woman who claims to be Laura Canady says she has proof you are not Philip Canady. She insists she can prove this — on Thursday."

"She's crazy!"

"Misguided, perhaps," Slade said dryly. "Or clever. But I suggest you wait and see what proof she brings forth."

The blond man threw up his hands. "Oh, all right! But I've taken all I can from this woman. I'll wait until Thursday — not a moment longer!"

He put on his hat and nodded coldly. "Good

day, gentlemen!"

The silence settled in cold layers after his departure. Dr. Mays' voice was worried.

"I expected you'd call him a liar to his face, Gil."

"Why?" Slade's tone was innocent.

"Well —" Dr. Mays flushed and straightened abruptly in his chair. "Damn it, Gil! You must have known Philip Canady. And that marriage certificate you said Ben Hobbs gave you — the one I've got locked up here in my desk — it proves that Laura Canady was married to Philip. She should know if this man is an impostor —"

"She should," Slade agreed. He leaned over the desk, resting his weight on the palms of his hands. "But think a minute, Doc. Who's the law in Badwater? And what could Judge Selman do with that certificate — how much weight do you think it would have in a court of law here? I brought it into Badwater. It'll be my word that Ben Hobbs gave it to me. It could be a phoney, Doc. Even you don't know, but maybe I'm in cahoots with this Laura woman to get all of Starlight."

Doc let out a slow breath. He studied Slade, then shook his head. "I don't believe it, Gil."

"Thanks," Slade said dryly. He straightened. "Do me a favor, Doc. Stall this man. I've got a hunch he's going to be told to sell and be damned to me. Selman's out to get Starlight — and he'll settle for half as a beginning! Stall this jasper until Thursday night —"

107

"Why? What's going to happen Thursday? What's Laura got up her sleeve, Gil?"

"Arrant's old housekeeper." Slade took the telegram from his pocket and dropped it on the desk in front of Mays. "She knew Philip Canady almost as well as his father."

Mays read the telegram. "Sure, I remember Arrant mentioning her. Said he needed a woman around the place, to take care of him —"

"He wrote her, it seems. One of the boys got the telegram a few days after Arrant died — he remembered it yesterday."

Mays was grinning with unprofessional glee. "This sure will hand Selman a jolt." Then he brought his hand up to massage his jaw thoughtfully. "Who is this man, Gil? He isn't Philip Canady. But how did he know so much about Philip and the old Pitchfork spread? And that ring?"

"I don't know," Slade answered. He thought of this, and he saw the same answer form on the older man's face.

"Whoever he is," Slade stated calmly, "he knows that the real Philip Canady is dead."

Mays shrugged. "Arrant waited years for that boy. Talked about him a lot. Even to me, who didn't know him, he kept making excuses for the boy. But in between his words you caught the feeling that Arrant wasn't really fooling himself. Deep down he knew his boy was no good and that he would not show up — he had this conflict inside him, and in the end it killed him."

Slade looked away. The old hate stirred briefly and subsided. He found himself, for the first time in five years, able to think of Arrant Canady with detached clearness.

Canady was a hard-fisted, bluff man he had respected and liked; a man he would have trusted with his life. It was this betrayal that had hurt most —

"Maybe he died at the right time," Slade said enigmatically, and went out.

Frank Hobson, at the bank, greeted Slade with cool reserve. He was in his office, behind the walnut railing, a thin, balding man with a sharp, confident manner. He watched Slade settle into the armchair opposite him.

"Henry will bring in Mr. Canady's account," he said smoothly. "I'll be able to give you a definite picture of Arrant Canady's financial affairs —"

"What's the general picture?" Slade cut in. "Is Starlight in the red — or do I have anything to work with?"

Hobson leaned back, steepling his hands. There was a thin red line across the bridge of his nose, made by the gold-rimmed spectacles lying on the desk in front of him. He was the sort of man who took off his glasses when he felt annoyed or pressed. Slade noticed that he made no move to put them on.

"Arrant Canady had a note with the bank, but he paid it off several weeks before he died. He could have paid it off any time he wished —"

"Then Starlight's in pretty good shape?" Slade pressed.

"Well yes — I'd say that's true." Hobson shrugged. "Of course, before I can legally turn over any assets to you, Mr. Slade, I must have a clearance from the court —"

"Are you questioning the legality of Arrant Canady's will?"

Hobson flushed. "No, of course not. I was one of the witnesses. But there's the question of the other partner, Mr. Slade. Until that is cleared up, I'm afraid I can't give you a free hand with Canady's bank account."

Slade leaned back. "I understand." He reached for his Bull Durham sack, and Frank Hobson said: "May I offer you a cigar — a real Havana?" He pushed a cigar box toward Slade.

Slade selected one and lighted up. "I need more hands at Starlight," he said bluntly. "I may not have time to wait until the question of Philip Canady or his wife is settled. It looks like a bad winter, and unless I resign myself to taking a bad loss in cattle, I'll have to have more riders."

Hobson pushed his hands apart in a gesture of sympathy. "Much as I would like to help you —" he began.

"Perhaps we can get around the difficulty in another way," Slade said. "Can I borrow money, with my share of Starlight as collateral?"

Hobson studied him a long moment. A slow smile smoothed the harsh lines around his mouth. "I see no reason to refuse a loan on that basis, Mr. Slade. I'm satisfied concerning your legal rights at Starlight."

"Then I'll sign the necessary papers now," Slade said. "For twenty-five hundred — ?"

Hobson grinned. "You work fast, Mr. Slade."

"There's no time for dawdling." Slade matched his grin. He watched Hobson take out papers from his desk, fill in along several lines, turn it around and push it toward him. "Your signature down there will do it."

Slade glanced at the note, signed it. He turned as Henry, the bookkeeper, came in with a ledger in his hands.

"Don't you want to go over Starlight's account?" Hobson asked.

Slade shook his head. "It'll keep." He took a deep drag on his cigar, removed it from his mouth and eyed it with frank appreciation.

"Best smoke I've had in years, Mr. Hobson."

The banker said: "I'll be right back." Slade settled back in the chair and surveyed the walnut-paneled room. Henry stood by the desk, his eyes roving nervously under his green eye-shade.

Hobson was back in a few moments with a sheaf of crisp bills in his hand. He handed them to Slade, who thrust them carelessly inside his coat pocket.

"Aren't you going to count it?"

"When I trust a man, I trust him until I find out differently," Slade said. He stood up and reached for his hat on the tree. "It's been a pleasure, Mr. Hobson."

Hobson leaned back in his chair after Slade left and folded his hands across his vest. He seemed quite pleased.

Henry shuffled restlessly. "You still want the book, Mr. Hobson?"

"Put it on the desk," the banker said. He reached for his glasses, and there was a smile in his pale brown eyes.

Chapter Ten

Laura Canady sat by the window, looking down on the flat ugly roofs of Badwater. The sky was leaden and an occasional snow squall beat tiny ice particles against the panes. The wintry blast reached into the room, through the frost-rimmed glass. She shivered and hugged her wool wrapper tighter about her.

She had spent a wakeful night napping in this chair. Although Dr. Mays had wanted to send a woman to spend the night with Matt, she had insisted on staying. She felt she owed that much to Kingston.

Matt had been restless most of the night; she had changed his bandage twice. But his temperature had remained normal; she had kept him covered, and toward morning he had fallen into a deep sleep.

She sat in the chair now, staring at the glass, not seeing the town or listening to the cold wind. She was tired. But a strange excitement stirred in her, just below the surface of her fatigue.

Gilbert Slade's visit had left her with hope, and with this odd feeling of exhilaration. It was more than the hope of gaining Starlight, which in the beginning had represented security for her and for her son Tommy. She had desperately wanted to belong somewhere, wanted Tommy to grow up in a place he could call home.

She felt an ache creep into her neck muscles. She folded her arms on the sill and put her head down on them. But the tall, rangy man with the quiet, unsmiling manner remained in her thoughts. She tried to analyze her feelings — tried to understand the sudden pulse of excitement in her. And, understanding, she drew back from it, denied it.

Once she had felt like this about another man — a boy, really; a handsome blond boy who had talked to her of excitement and cities and far away places. He had talked convincingly, and she had been young and at a point in time and development when she had listened.

He kept talking and promising up to the day he ran away. It was the day after she had told him she was pregnant. He had gone still, his face suddenly remote and white, as though she had just told him a catastrophe had occurred. Then he had laughed and said everything was all right. And the next morning he had been gone. . . .

The door opened and a plump, ruddy-faced woman skirting the shady side of middle age came in. She came to a halt in the middle of the room, took off her ancient, flower-decked hat and scratched through gray hair with an absentminded gesture.

"I knocked," she said briskly, "but you must have been asleep."

Laura stood up. "I'm sorry, Mrs. Fulman. I

must have been day-dreaming."

Mamie Fulman gave her a searching look. "I wouldn't have given you a penny for your thoughts then," she said. "You didn't look happy, girl."

"I'm tired."

"Of course, of course." Mamie nodded. She had a cheerful, motherly way about her. She had been widowed twice, borne eleven children, raised seven. She seemed to have a boundless energy and an optimism nothing could damage.

"Dr. Mays asked me to come over," she explained. "He thinks you should go home now and get some rest. He'll be in to see Matt a little later."

"It's nice of you to do this," Laura said gratefully.

Mamie was at bedside, tucking in the comforter. "Don't you worry about Mr. Kingston," she said. "I've taken care of wounded men before. Patched my first husband up five times before he was killed."

"I'm sure he'll be all right now," Laura said. "It's just that I felt responsible for him. If it hadn't been for me —"

"Bosh!" Mamie cut her off. "It's time you learned some things about men, girl. They're always fighting. They get restless when they go too long without a fight. Now take my oldest boy, Mike. Real chip off the old sod. Has to get his juices fermenting, he says, or he feels poorly."

Laura's smile was weak.

"Not that I approve of it," the widow said. "But sometimes that's the way it has to be. A man can back away from trouble only so far; then he either has to face up to what's pushing him or run."

"Matt wasn't running from anything," Laura said. Her tone was defensive, and she saw Mamie smile knowingly, and it occurred to her that most people in Badwater thought there was something more than just an employer-employee relationship between Matt and her.

The thought brought a wave of resentment flushing her face. Matt was a kind employer, a loyal friend — she felt nothing else for him. Besides, she was in no position to think of marriage — she was still Philip Canady's wife. And thinking of the boy she had married, she was surprised how little emotion she felt. There was no longer even hurt — only a vague feeling of pity.

She discarded the wool wrapper and put on her coat and hat and stopped by the dresser mirror. The face that stared back at her under the jaunty hat was peaked. She was twenty-three, but she looked older. The unwilling thought came to her that Gil Slade had seen her like this, and despite herself it mattered.

"I'll be back tonight," she said to Mamie, who was settling in a chair and reaching in her bag for her crochet.

"Don't have to," the older woman said. "I've got no one to worry about at home. But you have

116

a little boy. Go take care of him."

Laura went.

Matt wakened a few minutes later. He saw Mamie and closed his eyes again. But she had seen him. She came and stood by the bed and laid her palm against his forehead.

"Disappointed?"

He opened his eyes. "No. I can't expect her to stay here always."

"I see that bullet hasn't affected your common sense," Mamie said. "How's the shoulder?"

"Hurts," Matt muttered. He moved the fingers of his right arm. The pain tightened his lips. "Where's Doc Mays?"

"In his office. He says you'll be all right. Up and around in no time. Might even get next week's *Gazette* out," she lied cheerfully.

"Don't joke with me, Mamie," Matt growled. He had known this woman as long as most people in Badwater. She and her husbands had provided copy for many a *Gazette* edition.

"It all depends on how eager you are to get up," Mamie said. She stood by the bed, hands on her hips. "My first husband was shot five times. He never stayed in bed more than a day. Claimed most people died in bed —"

"I remember Tim," Matt cut in wearily. "He cut a fuse too short, and the dynamite blast got him."

"There wasn't enough of him left to make a decent burial," Mamie said unctuously. "But if

117

there had, he'd have tried to get up and walk home. That's the kind of man Tim was."

Matt hitched himself up on his pillow. "The man who shot me — he still in town?"

"Has a room right down the hall," Mamie answered. "But I don't think he's in —"

"I don't want to see him!" Matt snarled.

"Then why did you ask?" Mamie snapped.

Matt took a grip on his wrath. Laura Canady had denied the man was Philip Canady, but doubt remained. What if she had been lying all along? What if she had known Philip only well enough to get the idea she could get away with passing herself off as his wife? Perhaps she had come here in the hope Arrant would take her and her son in on the strength of her story. . . .

He felt this doubt take hold of him, and while he felt disloyal he could not rid himself of it.

"He claims he's Philip Canady," he muttered. "But Laura says he isn't."

"She should know," Mamie said firmly. She looked more closely at Matt. A good man. An honest man. But her first husband, Tim, had expressed a blunt opinion of Kingston:

"Nice fella, that newspaperman, Mamie. But no gumption. A man who sets on both sides of the fence generally winds up getting his danged butt shot off!"

She often repeated Tim's observations, although she had seldom agreed with any of them. But in this case she felt that her first husband had been right about Matt.

Matt would fight for a cause; he was no coward. But he had the bad habit of seeing all sides of a question, and often this immobilized him. He was therefore a man plagued by doubts. And in this frontier community, where violence was often the only arbiter, a man with doubts stood in the middle and was the target of all.

"Lay still," she ordered, and pulled the covers down from under Matt's chin. He was naked to the waist, his chest and shoulder swathed in bandages. His wound had stopped bleeding.

"Humph!" She tucked the covers around him again. "No need to change that bandage. The doctor said he'd be along soon. I expect he'll want to take a look at the bullet hole."

Matt's face mirrored his relief.

"You needn't look so happy," she snorted. "I've probably bandaged as many bullet holes as Doc Mays. A wad of chewing tobacco, or a shot of forty rod whiskey poured over that hole, would get you up in no time —"

She turned as someone knocked. "Yes — it's open," she called out.

Slade came into the room. He closed the door and made a quick search of the room. He saw that Matt was awake and scowling. He put his attention on the frowning woman standing by the bed.

"Sorry, ma'am," he apologized. "I thought Mrs. Canady was still here."

"She's gone home to get some sleep. What can I do for you?"

"I didn't want to disturb Mr. Kingston," Slade said. "But seeing as how he's awake and looking rational, I'll talk to him."

Matt hitched himself up higher on the pillow. "Mr. Slade," his voice was not friendly, "I can't see what business you can have with me —"

"Perhaps you've heard that Arrant Canady left half of Starlight to me," Slade interrupted. His voice was short. He knew the reason for Matt's apparent hostility, and he thought the man a fool.

"No." Matt tried to sit up, winced at the sudden pain it caused him. Mamie moved up close and stuffed another pillow under his head.

"It's true," Slade replied. "But that isn't why I'm here. Not to discuss my ownership of Starlight with you. I've been out to the ranch. I find I need more hands. I came to see you about putting an ad in your paper —"

"There isn't going to be any paper," Matt said. His voice was bitter.

"I understand." Slade nodded. "I was here to see you earlier. Mrs. Canady explained what had happened. But I had a brainstorm after I left. Setting up type for a flyer shouldn't be too much of a job. If Mrs. Canady would be willing, I'd like to run off about fifty. I'll distribute them myself —"

"No!" Matt's voice was adamant.

Slade looked steadily at the unshaven, gaunt-faced man on the bed. "Why? What have you got against me, Kingston? Starlight?"

"Maybe."

"Or Laura Canady?"

Matt's eyes darkened. "Leave her out of this!"

Slade smiled coldly. "It's your paper," he said. "But I thought you were against Crescent — not Starlight!"

"I back who I please," Matt said. His voice was harsh. "Anyway, you'd only be wasting your money. There isn't a man in Badwater who'd ride for Starlight, knowing how Judge Selman stood on the matter."

"I'll do the hiring for Starlight," Slade said flatly; "not Judge Selman."

"I didn't think so," Matt snapped. "You're not the only boss at Starlight." He knew he was playing this small, being petty. But he felt compelled to it. The confidence in this rangy man angered him — his own doubts about Laura plagued him — he wanted to lash out at somebody.

"I'm sure you're aware that Philip Canady has arrived in Badwater."

"A man who claims to be Philip Canady is in town," Slade admitted. "But he isn't Arrant's boy. And he isn't running Starlight yet."

Matt slid down slightly on his double pillows. "You sound almighty sure he isn't Philip Canady!"

"Aren't you?"

Matt licked his lips. "I — well, he showed up with a lot of proof."

Slade read the struggle in the man's face, the weakness in the man's eyes. Matt was one of those men who were never sure of themselves, or of those they loved. He wanted Laura Canady, but he would never get up the courage to ask her. And now he would never be sure she had ever been married to Philip. He felt sorry for this man — and sorrier still for Laura Canady.

Slade shrugged. "Well, it's too bad I couldn't do business with you, Mr. Kingston." He nodded to Mamie and started for the door.

"It won't do you any good," Matt grumbled. "But if Laura's willing, you can tell her it's all right with me."

Slade turned. He had been right about this man. Even in this matter he couldn't stick by his guns.

"Thanks." Slade's voice had a dry tinge of contempt he couldn't hide. He put on his hat and went out, closing the door behind him.

Mamie Fulman looked at Matt and slowly shook her head. . . .

Chapter Eleven

Nick Pathias had been expecting the rider. He was out behind his shed, skinning the deer he had shot earlier this morning, when his Indian wife alerted him. She came out of the back door of the roadhouse and made a quick motion toward the north trail. Her brown face was stolid and uncomplaining. She turned and padded back across the frozen ground and disappeared inside the house.

Nick drove the skinning knife into the shed wall, wiped his bloody hands on his trousers and picked up the shotgun he had propped against the tree trunk. He started to walk back to the house, leaving the half-skinned carcass hanging from the tree.

He saw the rider on the trail. He didn't break his stride, or give any indication he was worried. But he made sure there was only one man on the trail, and he knew that man, before he walked into the house. He went through the kitchen, ignoring his wife's questioning look, and into the bigger room that served as bar and general store.

He walked behind the plain varnished counter and placed the shotgun within easy reach. He wiped a glass clean and set it on the counter and was reaching for the bottle of raw whiskey when the rider pulled up at the hitchrack.

He had the shot poured when Pete Cajun came inside.

The half-breed was cold. He walked over to the stove and stood awhile, warming up, his dark face impassive. The shapeless coat he wore hid the knife in the sheath at his belt and the gun in his holster. He was a wiry, ageless-looking man, noncommittal and wordless. He was a man born with a handicap and resigned to it. The limits of his world were narrow and violent, and he did no thinking beyond it.

Nick kept wiping his glasses. Nick had his own reasons for burying himself in this lonely canyon. He had more ambition than Pete Cajun, and often he fretted at his confinement here. But he valued life more, and he was not that much of a gambler. He knew what awaited him in New York, from which he had fled. . . .

Pete finally left the stove. Nick knew better than to push this man. The half-breed walked over to an open showcase where several hand axes caught his eyes. He hefted one, grunted softly, set it aside and came to the bar and reached for his whiskey glass as though he had just left it standing.

Nick said: "Hello, Pete."

The half-breed grunted. He took his drink as though it were medicine, blinked once, wiped his lips with his sleeve.

Nick felt uncomfortable. He knew what Pete was after, but he wanted the man to ask. But

Pete Cajun merely pushed the glass back to him for a refill.

"Heading south?" Nick ventured.

Pete lifted his shoulders. He drank the next one with the same sense of taking bitter medicine. But this time it seemed to loosen his tongue.

"I'm looking for Joe and Red," he said.

"They were here," Nick admitted.

"You have Red's cayuse?"

Nick put his palms flat on the bar top. "Sure. You can have him, Pete. But I want to keep that Starlight animal, the one Ben Hobbs rode."

Pete's eyes glittered. "You keep him." He nodded. "But the boss wants to know what happened to Red and Joe."

Nick came around the bar and walked to the window. He motioned for Pete to join him.

"Out there," he said, jabbing his finger against the pane. "There's two graves up on the point, past the end of the corral, Pete. It took me half a day to dig them. I still got blisters on my hands." He paused. "Joe Yader and Red are in them."

Pete's eyes were bland. "Boss wants to know. Who killed them?"

Nick didn't answer right away. He walked back to the bar, and this time he poured himself a drink.

"Some jasper I never saw before," he said. "Big feller, walked with a slight limp. I thought he was the man Joe and Red were waiting for — they were in the kitchen when he came in. Then

Ben Hobbs showed up a little later. He was already shot. I figgered out later that Joe and Red must have run into him before, but he got away from them. They got in here about an hour before he showed up —"

Nick poured another drink for himself and for Pete.

"Joe and Red didn't figger on this big joker. But he seemed to know Ben. Joe and Red thought he'd stay out of it." Nick shrugged. "Better tell the judge this jasper's dangerous, Pete. Real fast with a gun —"

Pete said nothing. He picked up his glass, eyed it with brooding respect.

"They finished Ben," Nick went on. "But before he died Ben handed that big stranger an envelope. I heard him tell the hombre to make sure it got to Arrant Canady."

"Canady's dead," Pete said. He gulped the raw whiskey without blinking an eye this time. He had found out what he had been sent for without running into trouble. He could back-track the man who called himself Smith to a place where his real identity was known, but he didn't think Judge Selman wanted him away that long. And he didn't think that it would matter, anyway.

He had learned what had happened to Red and Joe, and that the big man knew Ben Hobbs. And more important, Smith had the paper Joe and Red had been ordered to get.

The judge would want to know that!

The whiskey was burning in his stomach now, and the ride back would be a cold one. Pete reached for the whiskey bottle. The judge could wait another day. . . .

Gritty snow fell softly in the alleyway behind the Open House. It whispered and slithered along the building, tapping gently at the window of Judge Selman's private office.

Big Bill Talley stood motionless, looking down at the slender, frowning figure behind the desk. It was just past noon, but the gray murk outside filtered weakly through the small window.

Judge Selman had lighted the small lamp on the desk. But he sat back, away from the bright circle of light, his face in the shadows. On the wall behind him the marshal's enormous shadow flickered.

"He's got something up his sleeve, Judge. He's doing a lot of moving around, too. He left Doc Mays' office and headed straight for the bank. Then he came out and went up to Kingston's room in the hotel. He stayed there a few minutes, then came out and headed for Ma Crane's Kitchen."

The lawman's big hands knotted, and he leaned his weight on his knuckles as he bent over the desk.

"He came out of there with that Canady woman and went straight to the *Gazette*. They're up to something, Judge —"

"Worrying is my department, Bill," Selman cut him off. "It doesn't suit you." He ran his long thin fingers down the edge of his coat. "Arrant Canady pulled a neat trick when he left half his spread to this stranger. Kept the secret well, too. Neither Doc Mays nor Frank Hobson breathed a word about this fellow Arrant was expecting."

"Maybe he ain't in old Canady's will at all!" Talley snarled. "Maybe the doc and Hobson just rigged up a phoney will to include this jasper. He don't scare easy, and he's fast with that gun —"

"Very fast," Walter Selman agreed. His eyes had a dark, brooding look. "But I don't think Doc Mays and Frank Hobson would take the risk. I don't see what *they* would have to gain by ringing in a gunslinger for Starlight." He shook his head. "No, I'll go along with the idea that Arrant Canady knew what he was doing. He wanted to save Starlight for his boy, Philip. But he knew that the only way to save it for him was to hand half of it over to some hardcase with a fast gun; someone he could trust to give his boy a fair shake." His lips curled. "It isn't going to do him any good, though. No good at all. After tonight I'll be half-owner of Starlight — and we'll see who runs Canady's spread!"

Talley said grimly: "He won't scare, Judge. We'll have to kill him!"

Selman shrugged. "In due time, Bill."

Talley snorted. He straightened and made a

gesture toward the door. "I'll drift out again and check on him. All I want is one thin excuse to lay my hands on him again." He fingered the badge on his coat, and his lips pulled in tight against his teeth. "One excuse so I can get him cornered in a cell without that gun of his!"

Selman smiled sympathetically. "When you do, I'll see that you get a raise in pay, Bill."

"That I'll do for nothing," the marshal snarled. He fumed and headed for the door and Selman called:

"Stop by the hotel and tell Philip Canady I want to see him. Right away." He paused to let this sink in. "Tell him to come down the alley and use my back door."

The lawman nodded. "He'll be here." He closed the door and went out, silent as a big cat and almost as deadly.

Selman waited. He leaned back in his chair and lighted a cigar and went back over the years to his meeting with the man he was waiting for. He would have to be careful with this man.

He closed his eyes, lulled a little by the warmth from the small pot-bellied stove in the corner. A stick of wood cracked sharply, and oddly enough, for the first time in years, his thoughts were of home. The path across the snow-covered field to the small knoll was brilliantly sharp. . . . It was the path he took from the farmhouse to school, five miles away.

A thin, tall boy appeared on the knoll, book tucked under his arm, wet to the knees from scuffing through the snow. Selman had a good look at the boy as he stopped on the rise to look down at the farmhouse below . . . narrow, flushed face, bright eyes, eager smile. He always waved from this point — he started to wave now. Then he saw the look on the boy's face change — saw terror strike deep in his eyes — heard the muffled sob.

The doctor's buggy was drawn up by the barn — and alongside it was the black, ominous funeral wagon of Jonas Baker.

His mother had been sick a long time, but the little boy on the knoll had never really felt she'd die. . . .

The memory came back to jar him. He straightened slowly and found that his cigar was dead. He crumpled it in the ash tray, and noticed with surprise that his hand was trembling.

At ten years a boy's whole life still lies before him; at forty a man looks back with bitter regret.

The boy was named Walter Selman — but he had little in common with the man he had become.

However, for an unguarded moment he had taken a glimpse back in time — and found no answer there, just as he had found no answer to his sobs as he had looked into his mother's still face.

The knock on the back door seeped into his awareness. He took a long breath, and the thirty years that separated him from that frightened, lonely boy crashed between them. . . . There was a hard, cold look in his eyes as he turned to the door.

The knob turned slowly, stopped.

"Come in," Selman said.

The door opened, and the man who had passed himself off as Philip Canady slipped inside and closed it quickly behind him. He stood with his back to the wall, his eyes searching the gloomy shadows, finding the man in the chair just outside the bright circle of lamplight.

He chuckled softly. "I started to come in. Then I remembered you were always as nervous as an old maid about anyone coming up to you without warning, Walter. So I knocked."

"You've acted pretty nervous yourself, Willy," Selman said coldly. "Did you have to shoot that fool Kingston?"

Willy Ames shrugged. "I didn't come to this God-forsaken country to get into a fist fight, Walter." His smile was humorless. "Your offer didn't include my taking a beating."

"From Matt Kingston?" Judge Selman shook his head. "You didn't get that soft since I last knew you, Willy."

Ames came away from the wall. He was dressed in the latest style; he looked impressive, cool, poised, sure of himself. Willy Ames could be broke and suffering from a toothache and he would still give that impression, Selman knew.

He watched the gambler take a small cigar from a silver cigar case and light up.

"He looked pretty big," Ames said casually. "And I knew he had to make a showing for that girl he was with. Philip's wife, wasn't she?"

"So she claims." Selman nodded. His voice was without warmth.

"You don't have to pretend with me," Ames said coolly. "I've seen her picture enough times, heard Philip talk about her, to recognize her as soon as I came down the stairs. She's Philip's wife all right. He left her, but he couldn't help talking about her —"

"He did a lot of talking, I remember," Selman said. "That's all he was good for."

"He wasn't much of a man," Ames admitted. "I knew Philip Canady pretty well. I cleaned him of his last dollar at the roulette wheel I ran in the Blue Dragon. Funny thing, like most wild kids, he thought he could beat the wheel. When he was broke, he hung around the place. I took pity on him and let him sleep in my room, bought him a few meals." Ames shook his head. "No, he wasn't much of a man. And I wasn't too surprised when he was killed. He was asking for it. He had one big weakness — if you have to separate them. He fancied himself a lady-killer. I warned him to keep away from the Creole dancer. Her husband was a Seminole. He didn't talk much, but he carried a switch knife with a seven-inch blade —"

"The devil with Philip Canady!" Selman broke in harshly. "He served his purpose. You're Philip Canady now, at least until you sign this

132

bill of sale and get out of town —"

Ames flicked ash from his cigar into Selman's ash tray and picked up the paper the judge pushed across the desk to him. He read it with a smile spreading across his handsome face.

"Just half of Starlight, Judge? Why, I thought I was going to inherit all of that big spread."

"Half will be enough," Selman growled. "Just sign, and I'll get you the money."

Ames made no motion to pick up the quill pen Selman held out to him. He put his eyes on the bill of sale. "You don't know the lift it gave me, Walter, inheriting a big spread like Starlight." He chuckled harshly. "Cattle baron Ames, instead of gambler Ames, con man Ames." He slid the bill of sale back on the desk.

"I've got three clean shirts in my bag in a hotel room I can't pay for," he said harshly, "and exactly two dollars in my pockets."

"I promised you three thousand!" Selman snapped. "You can buy all the shirts you want with that."

There was a clipped warning in Selman's tone that reached through to Ames, stemmed the tide of greed in him. He shrugged. "Sure, I'll sign. But you can't blame me for wondering, Walter. I thought I was going to inherit all of Canady's spread —"

"Old Arrant Canady didn't think enough of his kid to hand over all of Starlight to him," Selman said. "Seems he cut in some gunslinger for a half-share."

133

"I met him," Ames recalled. His eyes shadowed. "I got the feeling he was holding something back. I have a strong hunch he knew the real Philip Canady."

Walter Selman got to his feet. He was as tall as Ames, but slighter and more nervous. He wheeled sharply to face the gambler. "Once you sign this bill of sale Slade can squawk all he wants!" he snarled. "I'll be half-owner of Starlight. And before the week is out I'll be the only owner!"

"Then you better get this Slade hombre first — and get him fast!" Ames agreed. "I met him today, in Dr. Mays' office." He reached over and butted out his cigar in the tray. "He's going to be a hard man to handle, Walter."

Selman stood very still. "I'll handle him," he said calmly. "Just sign that bill of sale!"

Ames felt a stubborn desire to take his time signing. He wanted to savor for a few days longer the feeling of ownership in something more solid than a deck of cards and three clean shirts.

"I was told to wait," he murmured, "until Thursday."

Selman started. He came into the lamplight now, his face tight and very hard. "Who told you?"

"This gunslinger — Slade."

Selman sucked in a harsh breath. His eyes went muddy, roiled by a quick anger.

"If you're thinking of a double-cross, Willy?"

"No double-cross!" Ames said quickly. He

134

was alert, his right hand up by the third button of his coat. He had forgotten how quick Walter Selman was to anger.

"It's just that I feel that it's worth more than three thousand to sign away my rights to Starlight," he said coldly.

"I made a deal for three — not a cent more!"

"The deal also said it involved nothing more than my coming to Badwater, passing myself off as Philip Canady, getting legal ownership of Starlight and then signing it over to you —"

Walter Selman stepped to the desk and pushed the paper toward the gambler. "That's still all there is to it," he said grimly. "Sign it!"

Ames shook his head. "Get this gunslinger Slade and I'll sign. Or else fork over five thousand dollars, Walter. He told me to wait — and I didn't like the look in his eyes when he said it. If I sign with him still alive, it'll be worth all of the two thousand more."

Walter Selman trembled on the brink of explosion. But he got control of himself.

"Be here tomorrow night," he said. His voice was almost a whisper; he didn't trust himself to speak normally. "Slade will be dead, or else I'll have the five thousand for you."

Ames grinned faintly. He had moved back out of the circle of light, and Selman didn't notice the thin beads of sweat on his face.

"No hard feelings, Walter. Just business." He walked to the back door, paused. "You might try finding out what Barnes wanted me to wait until Thursday for. He seemed pretty sure that something would turn up then; something that would back the girl's statement that I am not Philip Canady."

After Ames' departure Judge Selman moved restlessly. A bitter anger made him dangerous. He prowled like some mean-tempered ferret, stepping softly, moving like a shadow in the gloom beyond the desk.

He had gotten Ames down here, wiring him when he knew Arrant Canady was dying. It had seemed like a foolproof scheme. He had sent two men to head off Starlight's ramrod, Ben Hobbs, with orders to kill and bring back any evidence Ben might have picked up of Laura's marriage to Philip Canady.

With Ben Hobbs and Arrant Canady dead, there was no one in Starlight Basin who would be able to identify Philip Canady — except Laura. And she had nothing to back her statements.

But Arrant's dividing Starlight put a crimp in Selman's game. And Willy Ames, an old con man scenting money, was gambling for more.

Well, Selman thought bitterly, maybe Ames would get his five thousand dollars — but quite likely he wouldn't live long enough to get out of the Basin with it.

He heard the horse walk down the alley, its coming muffled by the snow. A moment later someone knocked — one hard rap, two quick ones.

Selman stopped pacing, turned to the door. His fingers drifted to the shoulder holster under his coat. Then he walked to the door and opened it.

Pete Cajun slipped inside, and the judge closed the door and locked it. The half-breed's face was impassive. He shook snow off his shoulders, then stood like some shaggy dog which had been let in out of the weather.

"What did you find out?"

"Joe and Red are dead." Pete's voice was monosyllabic. He went on to tell Selman what he had found out. "Nick said to tell you this big fella knew Ben Hobbs."

"What else did Nick tell you?" There was grim surprise in Selman's tone. He had been expecting something like this, but he was shaken as he reviewed the toll so far taken by Slade.

"Hobbs gave him an envelope." Pete was surprised at the way Selman was taking this, but he didn't show it. "Nick said Ben asked this big fella to get that envelope to Arrant Canady —"

Selman wheeled around and walked back to his desk. He stood in the light, angry and scowling. So Slade had the proof that Laura was Philip's wife? Why hadn't he used it? Or was he playing his own game here — hoping to get Starlight for himself?

Still, he had told Ames to wait until Thursday; practically ordered the gambler to wait. He must have made an impression on Willy, for the gambler was not easily frightened.

Maybe Slade had turned the marriage license over to Doc Mays. It might be this Laura was banking on. But why wait until Thursday?

It didn't make sense. But Doc Mays knew. And he was the weakest and most accessible link in this puzzle.

Selman began to smile. He walked to his small cupboard, took out a bottle of his private stock and two glasses. He filled both glasses and turned to extend one to Pete.

The half-breed hesitated a brief moment. He knew that drinking with Selman meant that the judge wanted something special.

But he felt a warm glow push away the chill of the long trail. It was good to be important enough to drink with the boss. . . .

It was after six when Pete left. It was dark outside, and the snow had quit. It had turned colder, and the fire in the stove had died down to a few glowing embers.

Selman stood by the door and stared at the rough map of Starlight Basin he had tacked on the opposite wall. The lamplight barely outlined it. Up in a corner of that map a small circle marked the location of Crescent; the rest of the area belonged to Starlight.

Selman weighed the implications of what Ames and Pete Cajun had told him. The conclusion was inescapable. Arrant Canady, knowing he was dying, had hired a gunman to hold Starlight for him. He could almost hear the hollow laughter of the man who had built Starlight.

A sneer, half defiant, half uneasy, spread across Selman's thin face. His right hand vanished. Flame tongued across his coat front. The three shots seemed to make one jarring crash in the small room. Then he lowered the .38 to his side and walked to the wall map and eyed the one ragged hole his shots had made in the circle marked Crescent.

Someone knocked cautiously on the door which opened into the gambling hall, but the judge didn't answer. . . .

Chapter Twelve

Dr. Mays returned to Badwater after dark.

After looking in on Matt Kingston, he had made three outlying calls which had taken the rest of the afternoon. His last stop had been at the Jonas place, where he had been treating the fourteen-month-old boy for worms. The baby was subject to convulsions and had not responded to the usual remedy. In desperation he had fallen back to what his aunt, back in Pennsylvania, had tried — a teaspoon of kerosene once a day.

He had found the Jonas baby improved, and the parents grateful, and Doc Mays pondered on this as he drove his buggy into the stable and left it with a stablehand.

Picking up his black bag, he reviewed the course of his day. He had taken a look at Kingston's wound, lanced three boils, sewed up a bad gash in young Killian's arm which Killian had said was the result of an accident while sharpening a sickle in his barn, but which Mays suspected was the result of a quarrel with his wife. George Killian was brutal when he drank. He was a disappointed, unhappy man who took out his frustrations on his wife, who did not take his abuse passively. Mays was of the opinion they would kill each other one of these days. . . .

He came out into the light of the street and hesitated. The rutted, snow-covered street was cheerless. . . . The wind had an icy cut. The lighted windows hinted at warmth inside, and they deepened his sense of loneliness. He walked slowly toward the office, meeting no one on his side of the street. At a point up the block he paused, noting that the *Gazette* was lighted up. It must be Laura, he thought, working to get out today's edition of the *Gazette*. He felt kindly to this woman — not just because she was alone and with a little boy, but because she had made no scenes, raised no outcry, when Arrant Canady had turned her away from Starlight.

He stood on the walk and remembered that day, and he shook his head, feeling dispirited and tired. He had sided with Ben Hobbs in the case of this girl; he had felt then that Arrant Canady was blind to any failing in his boy. Ben Hobbs had proved Laura right, but it had been too late for Canady. And Ben had not lived to see the outcome.

He felt in his pocket for a cigar and found none and stood a moment longer, unable to make up his mind whether to cross the street and say hello to Laura or go home. The icy wind sent small puffs of loose snow across the deep ruts. He shivered and remembered the bottle of whiskey in his office.

His steps were quick as he went down the street. He went up the side stairs to his office, his feet crunching on the hard-packed snow. He steadied himself with a hand on the railing — the cold reached through his gloves.

The office was warm. Old Bledsoe, who ran the tailor shop below, must have kept the stove going, he was thankful to the old man for it. He walked to the leather, sprung-seat chair and sat down, not even taking off his coat. The heat came to him, thawing him out, and the tiredness reached deep into his bones.

He sat there, staring at the print of New York's Hudson River with Fulton's steamboat puffing upstream. But no feeling of anticipation came to offset the weariness in him. When Arrant Canady and Marshal Brill had been alive he had looked forward to these evenings, interrupted as they sometimes were with emergency calls.

But now there was no one. He had made no other close friends, and he was not the kind to take refuge within himself. He had no real sense of dedication to his work, although he was an able practitioner.

The heat got through to him, deep down and he rose heavily, discarded his hat and coat and gloves and loosened his tie. He stood and ran trembling fingers through his thinning hair, then turned to the cabinet and took out the whiskey bottle. He had not touched a drop until Arrant Canady died; now he knew he'd drift again, a small, aging man with a black bag and nowhere to go.

He was on his second drink when he heard the

door open and close softly. He turned his head, frowning at the interruption — he didn't want to see anyone tonight.

Pete Cajun crossed to his chair in three long strides. The point of his long knife touched May's neck just under his left ear. The shock held him motionless, glass in hand.

"No noise, Doc," Pete whispered. "Just listen."

Mays inclined his head slightly.

"Judge Selman wants to know what will happen Thursday. What is it Mr. Slade knows?"

"Nothing. I don't —"

The knife point pressed into the side of Mays' neck, bringing a tiny trickle of blood. He shrank away, and his glass dropped from nerveless fingers. The liquor splattered across the floor boards.

"What is it, Doc? Why did Slade tell Philip Canady to wait until Thursday?"

Doc Mays hesitated only a moment. He had no real stake in Starlight; he no longer felt himself a citizen of Badwater. He didn't really care what happened here.

"In my desk —" His voice was a croak.

"Get it!"

Mays turned his gaze to the dark, brutal face of the half-breed. The blade didn't move. He got up and walked to his desk, and Pete was behind him like a shadow. The menace of that blade made the doctor's knees rubbery.

He leaned against the desk to support himself,

and pulled open the side drawer with one hand. It was warm in the office, but it was more than heat that brought the sweat out over his face. He found the key under the small ledger, and with it he unlocked the center drawer. The envelope with the certified copy of Laura's marriage lay in plain view, but Cajun didn't know what it was, and Mays picked up the telegram Slade had left behind and closed the drawer.

He pushed the message across the desk, and Pete read it.

"Who is this Martha Upton?"

Mays cleared his throat. "That's Arrant Canady's old housekeeper. She lived at Pitchfork for years, right after Canady's wife died. She practically raised Canady's boy, Philip. She's due in at Siding Thursday, at one o'clock —"

"Yeah?"

There was no holding back. The half-breed was bent over the desk, waiting. Mays wished he had not dropped his drink — he needed it to keep his knees solid.

"That's what Gil Slade and Laura Canady have up their sleeve, Pete. Martha can positively identify Philip Canady. If the man who came to town posing as Philip is an impostor, she'll know it."

Pete grinned. "The judge will be glad to know this," he said. He thrust the telegram into his pocket. The clock on the wall suddenly banged out six strokes, the metallic notes jarring the quiet.

Mays started to back away. "That's all I know, Pete. That's why Slade told him to wait until Thursday —"

Cajun's grin remained plastered on his lips. It had no mirth — in Mays' mind it was like a gargoyle's grin. Pete moved toward him, not saying anything. The doctor kept backing up, slowly, until the wall stopped him. His eyes grew wide. The half-breed wasn't going to kill him? Not in cold blood? For no reason — ?

The blade went in fast, punching in just above the doctor's belt buckle. Mays' mouth sprang open, like a hinged trap. But no sound came out. He raised his hand to his stomach. The pain was like fire spreading through his insides. He locked his fingers over the cut and his eyes bulged. He took a step toward the back-stepping half-breed before falling.

Pete Cajun wiped his blade on the doctor's coat. Then he locked the front door, turned down the lamp, and went out through the back door which led down into an alley. . . .

The scrawny, stuffed bird in the clock on the shelf over Matt's cluttered desk popped out and called Laura and Slade cuckoo six times. Then he ducked back into his hole, to wait slyly another half-hour before reappearing for his rebuttal.

Gil tied the bundle and stacked it and turned to eye the clock. "Wonder what he's got against

145

us?" he said, brushing his hair from his eyes. There was an easy grin on his face.

"Oh, he's just a cantankerous old bird who likes to heckle people," Laura replied. There was bright laughter in her eyes that made her appear young; she was alert and alive and it didn't seem possible that only a few hours ago she had been dead tired after a sleepless night.

"One afternoon Matt threw a handful of type at him, but he was too quick for Matt," she continued. "See, those scratches on the side, just under the glass —"

"Didn't know Matt could lose his temper," Slade said. "Somehow I got the impression he was too staid for that sort of thing. A Massachusetts Puritan who knows exactly what's good for him — and for everybody else, too."

"Oh, Matt's methodical," Laura admitted. "And he's from Massachusetts — I think he mentioned some place called Ayer. Trouble with Matt is, he tries to be too fair. Everybody's got a side, he believes — a man should listen to all of them. It helps fill up a newspaper. But it sure weakens his editorials."

Slade reached in his pocket for the makings. He had started on this job with some trepidation and with a certain cynical practicality. Laura had not seemed particularly pleased when he had asked her to help him run off the help-wanted flyers — obviously the little rest she had taken had not helped her much.

But gradually, as they had worked together,

she had loosened up. He had fired up the big pot-bellied stove, and they both seemed to thaw as the room warmed. He had never worked in a print shop before, and he had marveled at her dexterity in finding the proper type.

They had run off the flyers, and then Laura had mentioned what a shame it was that the *Gazette* could not come out on time. Matt had the issue locked up and ready to go — all that was needed was a willing hand at the press wheel.

"Why not?" Slade had said. "I think I owe Matt Kingston that much."

Now they had run off the flyers and the press run, and the sense of a job done relaxed them. Slade brought a match up to the cigaret in his mouth. It was a new sensation, this lightness he felt. His world had too long been colored by hate — it was strange to find himself loosening up, discovering a new sense of joy in just living. He felt Laura's nearness, and the sparkle in her eyes was contagious. He was suddenly aware that he was smiling with her, and he remembered that he had smiled very little since that afternoon Arrant Canady had tried to kill him.

"You like Matt?"

Laura's smile was still on her face as she lifted her eyes to him. "Why, of course. He's been wonderful to me. He gave me a job when I needed one badly. I arrived here with but a few dollars. Ma Crane was very kind, too. But Matt believed in me. He and Ben Hobbs. I think Dr. Mays did, too."

Ben's dead, Gil thought. *And Matt has his doubts. He doesn't believe in you all the way —*

But he didn't say it. It wouldn't be fair to tell her what Matt had said.

Fair? What were the rules between man and woman? Wasn't there a saying: *All's fair in love and war?*

It was then he realized he was in love with this woman. It came as a start, a realization that began in the pit of his stomach and spread through him. It was desire and wonder merging into a dream that had shadowy outlines of meaning. It held the hope of everything he had ever wanted without blueprinting it. Up to this moment Starlight had meant nothing more than a place to work, a challenge to keep in the face of Crescent's move to take the ranch over.

Now he was suddenly aware that it could mean *home!*

"Laura?" His voice was suddenly sober. "Are you in love with Matt?"

His question startled her. She searched his face, wondering at it — she was woman enough to recognize what she saw. Her breath quickened. Inside her the cold knot of cynicism, compounded out of anger and betrayal, vanished. There was a strength in Gil Slade that had never been in Philip — she knew she would never have to mother this man.

"No." Her voice was soft. "No."

He moved to her, searched her face and read

what he wanted to see in her eyes. The moment trembled in eternity — and was broken by the pounding on the door.

Slade turned, and Laura went past him to the door. A raw-boned, long-necked farmer stamped uncomfortably, glancing past her into the shop. "Thought I'd stop by for the paper 'fore I drove home," he said. He squinted at Slade. "Where's Mr. Kingston?"

"In bed, with a bullet hole in his shoulder," Slade said. "Been in town long, you'd have heard the news."

"Nobody said," the man muttered. "Just came in for flour an' things, an' Hosiah at the store was pretty busy. Didn't have time to talk, I imagine —" He nodded thanks as Laura handed him a paper. "This the new man Mr. Kingston hired?"

"You might call it that," Slade said. He closed the door after the farmer left, and Laura burst out laughing. "You make a fine hired hand, Gil."

"And you make a mighty pretty boss —"

The smile remained in her eyes, but deep down was the sobering remembrance that she was still a married woman, that she was still Phillip Canady's wife. It spoiled the moment for her.

"I'm hungry," she said. "They usually have fresh doughnuts and coffee at the café across the street. Sound good to you?"

"Sure does," Slade said. But he sensed the

change in her, and his own smile was a little bleak.

They were in the café when the news reached them. John Bledsoe, old and gray and round-shouldered from a liftetime bent over a sewing needle, came into the steamy eating house. He was looking for Marshal Talley.

The tailor turned to Laura when he saw her. His face was pinched, and behind his glasses his eyes had a dazed look.

"Dr. Mays . . ." he kept repeating. He came to the table where Laura and Gil sat. "Dr. Mays . . . he's dead . . ."

Laura gasped. Gil said quickly, "When? How did it happen?" He was getting up as he asked.

"Someone killed him — with a knife. Not more than ten, fifteen minutes ago —"

"I want to see him," Slade said.

"I'm coming, too," Laura put in firmly. She was getting her coat and hat. Her face was white.

Bledsoe looked around the café. The few customers at the stools looked startled. One of them said: "I'll go find the marshal."

Slade and Laura followed the little tailor to Mays' office. They went up the rickety stairs and into the office. Mays lay quiet in the area between desk and wall. He was on his back, and his mouth and his eyes were still open, as though he wanted very badly to speak to someone. Blood had stained his pants and his shirt and made a little thick puddle on the floor.

150

"I turned him over," John Bledsoe explained. "At first I thought he had just fallen —" He made a gesture with his hands. "I had heard him come in before six o'clock. I live just below. I didn't hear anybody else — just the doctor." He shook his head like a man in a dream. "I often came up here, kept his stove going when he went on his rounds. I came up a few minutes ago to tell him Mrs. Olsen wanted to see him about her rheumatism. The front door was locked from the inside. I went around by the back —"

Heavy boots tramped on the rickety outside steps. Laura was by the desk, her face bloodless. She turned to Slade. "All of them!" The words seemed to choke her. "All of them believed in me. Ben Hobbs. Matt. Now Dr. Mays —"

She stared into Barnes' hard face, sudden fear shaping her words. "You! They'll be after you next —"

The door opened and Marshal Talley tramped in. He was followed by a small group of curious townspeople who crowded silently into the doctor's office.

Someone started to close the door. Talley whirled. "Keep it open! Darn place's like an oven." He walked over to Gil, his jaw jutting belligerently. "What are you doing here?"

"Just leaving," Barnes snapped. He took Laura's arm. There was nothing he could do for Dr. Mays here.

He wondered if the killer had found the copy of Laura's marriage license. With Marshal

151

Chapter Thirteen

Marshal Bill Talley paused to read the notice tacked on the billboard in front of the general store and post office. He read it twice, hands thrust deep into his pockets, his head jutting belligerently. It was the help wanted flyer Slade Barnes had distributed throughout town and tacked up in various places.

Barnes had waited in the lobby of the Stage Hotel, Bill remembered. Waited until midnight, then turned in. Not a man had shown up.

Talley sneered as he reached out and tore the notice from the board, wadded it into a small ball and tossed it away.

Turning away, he caught sight of Willy Ames coming out of the hotel. The gambler moved briskly across the street, pushing against the icy wind. Badwater appeared more bleak than ever this late afternoon. The storm gathering over the Breakers was going to be a bad one. The snow squalls that had been hitting Badwater were but advance scouts for the main blow building up fast. Talley judged the storm would start before sunrise tomorrow.

Thursday. The day Arrant's old housekeeper was due in at the whistle stop depot of Siding. . . .

Talley's hands fisted. He had wanted a crack at Barnes since that first day in the Open House when Slade had humiliated him.

Ames came by on his way to the bank and nodded his greeting to the marshal. Talley knew Ames had an appointment with Frank Hobson to get legal title to a half-share in Starlight. And he knew that the gambler would be pressured into selling to Judge Selman before dark.

He turned away from the billboard, moving like some massive block along the walk. As town marshal, he kept the peace in Badwater. He was also Judge Selman's man, but few people seemed to resent this fact, or if they did, they kept their resentment from showing.

He turned into the Open House and walked through the pre-supper crowd to the bar. The lamps were already lighted, dimming the last gray smudge of daylight against the windows. Judge Selman stood by the far curve of the bar, dealing himself poker hands. He saw Bill Talley walk directly toward him and guessed what the marshal wanted. He scooped up the cards and thrust the pack into his pocket and turned to his office without a word.

Talley closed the door behind him.

Selman walked around his desk and settled in his chair. It was almost like the scene of the night before — but this time it was Selman who was calm and the marshal who moved restlessly.

"I reckon you know why I'm here," Talley growled.

Selman shrugged. "Slade?"

The marshal nodded. He reached up and tore the badge from his coat and held it between thick fingers. The principles behind that glittering piece of metal, the firm responsibility it implied, had never interested him. Only the sense of importance it had given him had pleased the big lawman.

"He'll have to come back to Starlight by way of Big Timber Trail," he said. "I'm going out tomorrow morning and wait for him."

Selman's tone was cold, disapproving. "Not you, Bill. I need you here."

Talley shook his bullet head like a stubborn bull. "Not this time, Judge. I want him!"

"I sent Walleye on ahead to Siding!" Selman snapped. "Let him handle Slade — and Arrant's old housekeeper. He'll be waiting there when Slade rides in tomorrow. Stay out of it, Bill!"

Bill's thick hands clenched. "No!"

The judge's hesitation was calculated, but the marshal did not notice. "Walleye's faster with a Colt than you are, Bill. Don't take on more than you can handle!"

The lawman's big fingers came together, twisting the badge into a shapeless bit of metal. "You're wrong, Judge! I don't think Walleye will stop him. But I will!" He tossed the hunk of nickel on the desk in front of Selman. "I'm not as good as Slade with a Colt," he snarled. "But a rifle will put me even, Judge!"

Selman leaned back in his chair. "I wish you

luck, Bill." He watched the big man wheel away; he sat quiet for a long time, listening to the noise beyond the door.

Some men you hired and gave orders to — others you led along by pride, letting them do what you wanted by questioning their ability.

With Walleye waiting for Slade in Siding, and Big Bill Talley keeping vigil on the return trail, the odds were all against Slade living to return to Badwater.

Siding was located on a small flat under the cold gray rock of the Breakers. Through the gritty flakes pounding him Slade heard the long lonely wail of an engine, carried to him by the shrieking wind.

The roan he rode snorted tiredly. Flakes of ice clung to the animal's eyelids. Slade peered through the snow.

"Sounds like we'll be a little late," he muttered to the cayuse. "But she'll be waiting at the station, I reckon."

He wondered a moment if Martha Upton would recognize him. He had known her for two years, an efficient, not too talkative, angular woman who had taken Philip's rudeness with stolid silence.

Meeting her here brought back the ugly memories of Pitchfork, but he was surprised to find that they no longer mattered. Laura Canady mattered now — and holding Starlight against Judge Selman.

Martha would be able to identify the man in Badwater as an impostor. It would ruin the legal gloss with which Selman had attempted to take over Starlight — it would leave Crescent's boss only one alternative. Force!

Gloomily Slade surveyed this possibility. A lot would depend on the loyalty of the six men he had left at Starlight — men who had owed allegiance to Arrant Canady, but not to Gil Slade, or a woman who claimed to be Philip Canady's wife.

He had spent yesterday at the ranch, taking stock. Arch Nelson had remained aloof — so had Hal Taylor. The others had seemed more friendly. But he had been heartened this morning when he left by Arch, who had come into the yard and watched him saddle the roan.

"Gonna be a bad one," Arch said, squinting at the dark blue mass over the Breakers. "Sure you don't want me, or one of the boys, along?"

"We're short-handed enough," Slade said. "And I've got a feeling Crescent might try to move in, Arch. If Selman succeeded in getting a bill of sale from the phoney Philip Canady, he might decide to ride up here and take over —"

Arch had licked his lips. "Let 'em. There's six of us here — and we've got six rifles —"

Slade thought of this now as he headed for Siding. Fifteen minutes later he rode into Siding's single street. Snow whipped in little white trailers across the road. A few horses huddled before the one saloon, pressing against each other for warmth. Ahead of Slade a wagon lurched like a gray ghost, heading out of town.

Slade cut left at the building line. Siding's station lay a quarter of a mile west of the small huddle of shacks. Corrals and smaller pens, built by Starlight to facilitate the loading of cattle, were strung out along the single track that rejoined the main line fifty miles west.

Slade pulled up at the station. A wooden platform, partially shielded by a sloping wooden awning, extended along the track side of the oblong box that housed the waiting room, telegraph office and freight shed.

A slim figure wrapped in a high-collared coat was standing at the edge of the platform, peering through the murk toward town. Slade dismounted and walked toward her.

"Martha Upton?"

The figure turned. A pair of dark, lively eyes looked up into his. The pert features, even more piquant under a ridiculous hat, were decidedly not what Slade had expected. She was not Martha Upton!

It was a young face, full-lipped, and even as he hesitated Slade caught a whiff of a delicate perfume.

"*Non,*" the girl laughed. "*Pas* Martha." Her voice had a pleasant French accent, almost caressing. "I am Mrs. Philip Canady, *monsieur.*"

Slade settled back on his heels. Midway down the platform a tall, bony woman stepped out of a sheltered doorway. "I'm Martha Upton," she called. "Are you from Starlight?"

Slade said: "Excuse me, Mrs. Canady," and started for the woman in the station doorway.

The younger woman caught him by the arm. "*Monsieur* — I, too, am going to thees Starlight Ranch —"

The rifle made a sharp crack above the snow-powdered wind!

Martha Upton gave a short, choking cry. Slade yanked his arm free of the girl's grasp and ran forward, drawing his Colt. The old Pitchfork housekeeper was in a limp, unshapely huddle, moaning softly.

Slade whirled as a bullet splintered the framing several inches from his face. His Colt spat a reply to the dimly seen figure dodging back behind a freight car standing on a short side track by the pens. The man staggered, but kept running, fading out of sight. . . .

Slade said: "Get the station man to help — get her inside!" to the startled, white-faced girl who had followed him. He cut across the platform and headed after the killer.

The man was a vague shape, just getting into the saddle of a black horse which had been left tied to the bars of the nearest cattle pen. Slade slipped on a snowslick rail as he cut down at the man.

The black horse screamed as Slade's bullet raked its ribs. Rearing, it unseated the man who had not yet settled himself in the saddle.

The killer scrambled to his feet. He got his

back against the pen bars, his rifle whipping up, flaring red and orange through the swirling snow.

Slade felt the slug pluck at his coat sleeve. Then his own Colt slammed its answer.

The small figure seemed to flatten against the bars. The rifle dropped first, sliding down into the snow. Then the man slid sideways, turning as he fell to bury his face in the cold whiteness.

Slade paused just long enough to turn the man over — stare into the thin hard face that death had frozen into a pained snarl. It was the face of one of the four men who had lined the bar in the Open House the day Judge Selman had held open court.

The station master, a short, pudgy man wearing a green eyeshade, was bending over Martha when Slade got back. He looked up at the tall, grim man. "She won't need a doctor," he said stiffly. "She's dead."

Slade's lips tightened. "Give me a hand with her," he said harshly. "We'll take her inside, anyway." Bending, he took his first look at the woman he had known well — in late middle age, with care-worn features. She had come a long way, he thought bitterly, to hold a rendezvous with death.

He felt fingers pluck at his coat sleeve as he deposited the body down on one of the hard benches inside the station. He turned impatiently.

Mrs. Canady said: "You work for Starlight, monsieur? Yes?"

Slade nodded.

"Then maybe you work for my husband, eh? Philip Canady?"

Slade's smile held irony. "I don't think your husband particularly cares who's working for Starlight," he replied. "When I left your husband he was planning to sell the ranch and return East."

"Oh!" The woman's dark eyes went wide and round. "I must get to heem. He must not do such a theeng. His poor papa —"

"His poor papa is dead," Slade said shortly.

The girl's "Oh!" sounded genuine. She looked around the dingy station while Slade spoke to the harassed station man. "Is there an undertaker in town?"

The man nodded. "Charley Lenger — veterinarian. He does embalming, too."

"See that he takes care of her. I'll send someone out from Starlight as soon as this storm blows over."

He started out the door before he remembered the girl. She was right behind him.

"You'd better stay here, Mrs. Canady," he said. "It's eleven miles back to Badwater, and the storm's getting worse." He smiled at the face the girl made. "I'm sure your husband will be over for you in the morning, when I tell him you're waiting for him."

Mrs. Canady shook her head. "Ah, but I am

161

afraid you do not know my husband, meester —"

"Slade," he said, grinning despite himself. "You can call me Gil."

Mrs. Canady smiled coquettishly. "I do not mind zee cold, Geel," she said, "if I ride weeth you. You are so beeg and strong, eh? You can call me Jeanne."

Slade shrugged. It had occurred to him that the man who called himself Philip Canady was not expecting this woman. He had a feeling that he was going to be a mighty surprised man.

"Do you ride, Jeanne? Saddle, I mean?"

She nodded. "But *oui!* I am a good horsewoman. In New Orleans I ride every day in zee park —"

Slade took her arm. "Come on. I'll see if I can rent a saddle horse for you in town!"

Chapter Fourteen

Big Bill Talley waited patiently, not minding the cold. Snow sifted down through the alder screen. It made soft slithering sounds like the patter of tiny feet through the branches.

The Big Timber Creek road curved along the south bank of the cold running stream. The alder clump where the marshal waited edged the road to Siding. Slade would have to pass within thirty feet of where Talley crouched.

Behind the big man, down in a small pocket walled in by the gray rocks of the ridge, was a cabin. Once it had belonged to a man named Jed Thomas. It had been deserted for more than a year.

He could have waited there in more comfort, but the way the snow was driving across the clearing, a man could ride along the road and never be seen from the cabin. Talley cursed harshly as snow sifted down into his collar.

His rifle was propped against the tree trunk at his feet. He kept his big hands in his pockets. He could have worn gloves, but he didn't want to waste time peeling them off when his man showed up.

He had been waiting three hours, sustained by the galling memory of the contemptuous manner in which he had been handled back in the Open House by a man at least forty pounds lighter.

Big Bill Talley had been king in Badwater. When he walked down the street men gave him room. No one had ever argued with him.

The snow drifted across the road in front of him. It was narrow here, hemmed in by the alder clump on one side. The road sheered off on the other, dropping fifteen feet to the dark gray, fretting waters of the creek.

Talley shuffled his feet against the numbing cold. Maybe Walleye had stopped Slade. The possibility, finally admitted, disturbed him.

Picketed behind him, his horse moved restlessly, shaking snow from its stringy mane. The animal whinnied a soft complaint.

Talley's patience was almost exhausted when he saw movement on the trail. Riders were forming like gray ghosts out of the swirling snow. Talley's breath rasped hot in his throat.

He saw the man he had been waiting for, partially covered by a smaller figure riding hunched against the wind. Talley lifted the muzzle of his rifle. Behind him, sensing equine companionship to lessen the misery of its long wait, his horse suddenly shrilled a welcome. . . .

For the last hours Slade had been thinking of the small cabin off the road ahead. He had spotted it on his way to Siding, and now, bucking a thirty-mile wind that was driving snow across that bitter-cold land, he decided to seek shelter within its sagging walls.

Alone, he might have pushed on through to Badwater. But he was concerned for the small, uncomplaining woman riding beside him.

He eased his roan back and leaned close to her scarf-muffled head. "How are you?" he asked.

The girl's impish eyes met his above the swathing of wool that covered her face. Her voice, muffled through the cloth, sounded cheerful enough. *"Bien."*

Slade moved an arm toward the dark clump of alders looming ahead of them. "There's a cabin just past those trees," he said. "I think we better hole up there until it stops snowing."

The girl twisted to peer toward the alders. Her mount lunged up as she jerked her bit reins. And in that moment a horse nickered from the dark trees — and a rifle blasted through them!

Jeanne Canady's mount took the slug through the head. It was knocked sideways, against Slade's roan, who lost his footing in the treacherous snow. The horse fell backwards, just as the rifle blasted again.

Slade slipped clear of the roan's weight. But Jeanne Canady's soft figure fell across him as he groped on hands and knees, momentarily pinning him down with her weight.

The girl was either hurt or had fainted. She lay across Slade, her weight pressing down on him.

Slade made no attempt to roll her off. He knew that any movement would bring another shot from his ambusher. He had one long chance in that swirling snow — the possibility that the killer couldn't have clearly judged the results of his two shots.

The roan had scrambled to his feet. Slade could see the trembling hind quarters of the stallion. Suddenly the roan snorted and lunged away, and Slade sensed that his ambusher was coming out of the timber to investigate.

The girl stirred on Slade. She moaned. Slade's body tensed. He was in a bad position to reach his Colt, and he knew any movement would bring a quick shot. He waited, eyes lidded, feeling a man bulk over him.

The girl's moaning changed to a startled outcry. Slade felt her weight lift and ventured to open his eyes, peering through slits at the man bending over him. He recognized the marshal of Badwater as Talley picked Jeanne up with one hand and carelessly tossed her aside.

He bent over Slade, the muzzle of his rifle swinging down. . . .

Slade's boots lashed out.

Big Bill cursed as his rifle flipped out of his hands and buried itself in the snow. He dropped down on Slade, a snarl ripping from his lips.

"Glad I didn't kill you just now! This way is better!"

Slade felt the man's big hands reach for his throat. The marshal's weight was a smothering thing. Desperation spurred Slade. He got a palm under the lawman's jaw and jammed upward with savage strength.

The big man's snarl changed to a surprised grunt. Slade heaved and rolled the man over. They scrambled up together. Talley charged in like an angry bear. He wanted to get in close to this man, use his advantage, his weight, his strength. He wanted to break this grim-faced man with his bare hands!

Slade's right hand stopped him, jerked his head back violently. It wiped the snarl from his face, left his mouth a red, broken mess. Talley shook his head like a stung grizzly and walked in, taking another solid blow that smashed his nose, half blinded him with his own spurting blood.

His massive arms locked around Slade. In a savage burst of strength he wrestled Slade clear of the road and started to stumble with him toward the embankment.

Jeanne Canady watched them battling in the snow. She started to drag herself back, felt something hard under her hand. She picked up Talley's rifle and sat cross-legged, eyes squinting against the stinging snow, and slowly levered a shell into the chamber. . . .

Bill was almost across the road when he stumbled. He and Slade went down together in a threshing heap. But the marshal was on top.

His voice burbled through his mashed lips. "I'm going to finish you for good this time!" His hands closed around Slade's throat.

Slade drew his legs under the marshal. His breathing was choked off; his lungs ached. He quit trying to break the man's grip on his throat. He got his two hands, palms upward, under the big man's chest. With a sudden burst of strength he kicked upward, shoving against that barrel chest at the same time.

The marshal's fingers tore free, furrowing the skin of Slade's throat. He flipped completely over Slade's head, sprawling precariously close to the edge of the road.

But Slade was spent. His neck felt broken, and he had difficulty breathing. A blind instinct made him claw to his knees. He started to fumble for his holstered Colt, knowing that this was his only chance. . . .

Talley got to his feet. He swayed like some huge, bloody bear, pawing at the blood in his eyes, peering to locate Slade. There was enough strength left in him to break Slade. A smothered snarl broke from his bloody lips, and he started forward.

The rifle shot stopped him in midstride. He stood still, twisting slowly to face the shot. The second whip crack stiffened him. He brushed a hand across his eyes, as though he were suddenly very tired.

Slade's Colt blasted heavily.

The impact of this heavier slug shoved Talley back. . . . He teetered on the edge of the embankment, but made no real effort to regain his footing. He dropped out of sight without a sound.

Slade remained on his knees for a while

longer. His lungs dragged in air with difficulty. He saw the girl come toward him, still holding Talley's rifle, and he was vaguely grateful to her. It was a full two minutes before he felt strong enough to stumble to his feet and shuffle to the embankment over which the lawman had disappeared.

Below him the rim ice close to the bank was broken. But he saw nothing else save the dark turbulent current sweeping downstream. . . .

Slade turned to the girl. Jeanne Canady was standing beside her dead mount.

"Mon Dieu!" she wailed. "My horse. I cannot walk to the town of Badwater, Geel!"

Slade wiped blood from his face. He felt tired, arm-weary, bruised beyond belief. He was in no condition to ride, either.

"The cabin's just off the road," he said, pointing. His voice was a croak, and it hurt him to speak. "And Talley's horse is picketed somewhere in those trees. We'll wait until the storm lets up. Might have to stay here all night. . . ."

Chapter Fifteen

The morning sun reddened the streets of Badwater like blood spilling along the white thoroughfare. The thirty-mile wind had piled snow door high against one side of Main Street, left the other swept clean. A wagon from one of the small spreads just outside town made ruts through the new snow as it came into Badwater. The driver sat stolidly, hunched in his greatcoat, his breath spuming white against the cold.

Four mounted men waited in front of the Open House. Al Cramer, Pete Cajun, Randy Sellers and Hal Eames — all that remained of Crescent's gun-tough crew.

The judge came out of his office, pulling skin-tight gloves over his lean long fingers. He carried a rifle under his arm and looked uncommonly bulky in his coat. There was no one in the gambling hall downstairs except a sleepy-eyed bartender named Sawyer — and Lee Whitehead, nursing the pain of his bullet-torn arm with whiskey.

Selman said: "We've waited long enough, Lee. Walleye and Talley should have returned by now."

He glanced toward the windows, a vague uneasiness in him. Slade hadn't shown up, either

— but Crescent's boss didn't feel satisfied. He would have given a thousand dollars to know what had happened out there in that storm yesterday.

"If Bill comes back, send him to Starlight," he told Whitehead.

Whitehead nodded. He trailed behind the judge and paused in the doorway. The cold prickled his liquor-flushed face.

Selman mounted the saddled horse Cramer was holding for him. Whitehead watched the contingent wheel, head for the south trail. Puffs of snow kicked up behind them. After a while Lee went back inside.

Sawyer poured him another drink. The bartender had little sympathy for Whitehead; he didn't show any now. He placed the bottle on the counter and growled: "Help yourself. Yuh got a good arm."

Lee was restless. The gnawing pain in his bandaged arm kept him on the move. He prowled from bar to window to front door.

He was halfway through the whiskey bottle when he saw riders come down the street. One of them was the rangy, unsmiling man he had encountered at Starlight. Slade! The other was a woman. He had never seen the woman before — but he had seen the horse she rode many times. It was Big Bill Talley's blue roan!

A wild hate twisted through his thin body, sidetracking the pain in his arm. Walleye and Bill had both failed! Slade had come back from

Siding — and the woman, although younger than he had expected, must be Martha, Arrant's former housekeeper.

Whitehead's left hand reached for his holstered gun; then he gave up. The distance was too great for a Colt, but not too long for a rifle! Turning, he ran for the judge's office, disregarding Sawyer's questioning growl. He knew there was a gun rack in the office. He picked out a gleaming Winchester and laboriously jacked a shell into position. Then he ran back across the big hall.

He reached the door in time to see Slade and the woman disappear through the door of the Stage Hotel, a block and a half up the street. He eased back against the framing, disappointment burning in his narrow face.

Then he settled back, cuddling the rifle under his arm. Slade would have to come out of the hotel sometime. . . .

Slade helped the girl off Talley's roan and up the steps of the hotel. The woman had taken the ride and the cold with uncomplaining fortitude, and Slade's admiration for her was genuine.

"Is Philip Canady in?" he asked the clerk.

The desk man nodded. "He's leaving on the noon stage, I understand. That is, if the stage hasn't been held up by yesterday's storm. I'll have someone call him for you —"

"No — I'll go up to him," the woman said,

smiling. "I'm *Mrs.* Canady."

The clerk's eyes rounded. But his tone remained respectful. "Number eleven — turn left at the head of the stairs. Far end of the hall, Mrs. Canady."

Jeanne turned to Slade. "I'm very grateful, Geel. Some day, maybe, I can thank you — eh *bien?*" She shrugged small shoulders and headed for the lobby stairs.

Slade looked after her. They had both been too tired to talk much last night, and what she had said had been guarded: just that she had married Philip Canady in New Orleans, and that only a few weeks ago Philip had learned that his father, who owned a big ranch out here, had been looking for him. Philip had come on ahead, while she disposed of some matters in New Orleans. She was to meet him here in Badwater.

Her story had sounded genuine, and if he hadn't known the real Philip Canady, he might have believed her. As it was, he had an idea that the man upstairs was due for a shock — and he wanted to be back before the fake Philip Canady recovered from his "wife's" visit.

He turned to the desk clerk who was eyeing the disappearing ankles. "Matt Kingston still in his room?"

The clerk shook his head. "He was moved to Ma Crane's place early this morning."

Slade nodded. He wanted to see Laura Canady anyway. It was time he told her the truth about himself — and about the certificate he had been given by Ben Hobbs.

He opened the door and stepped out, colliding with a chunky individual hurrying to get inside. The collision saved Slade's life.

He fell back against the doorway and heard a bullet splat into the wood over his head and dropped to the walk, rolling toward the hitch-rack. The outraged citizen gave a strangled cry of fright and crawled swiftly across the threshold into the hotel lobby.

The second slug didn't come immediately, which surprised Slade. He had no way of knowing that Whitehead was cursing pained, clumsy fingers as he tried to jack another bullet into place.

Slade rolled off the walk, under his roan's legs, just as the second bullet scoured the plank walk. Cuddling his Colt, he slammed a shot toward the door of the Open House where a puff of black smoke revealed the rifleman.

He received no answering fire, but that fact didn't relieve Slade. He couldn't stay where he was — a good rifleman could get into position and pick him off. He had to make a break — take advantage of the strange marksmanship of the man in the Open House.

Straightening, he made a dash for the alley separating the hotel from the building next to it. He made its protection without drawing a shot. . . .

Lee Whitehead had backed away from the door after the second shot. His face was white with the realization that he had trapped himself in his eagerness. Sawyer was cursing him.

"You goddam fool!" the bartender shouted. "You've brought that gunslinger down on our necks with yore goddam shootin'!"

Whitehead whirled. "Shut up!" he snarled. His face was wild with fear. Sawyer's mouth tightened sullenly. Stealthily he reached for the Colt he kept under the counter. He had never liked Lee Whitehead. . . .

Lee was backing toward the rear of the saloon, his eyes on the front door. He had levered another shell into position, and he held the stock of the Winchester hugged under his throbbing arm.

Sawyer called out harshly: "Damn you, Lee! Get out of here! I don't want that gunslinger bustin' in here —"

Whitehead whirled, brought his ride up. "Another word out of you," he snarled, "an' I'll —"

Sawyer shot him between the eyes. It was a good shot for the barman. He still had the Colt in his hand, resting on the counter, when Slade came in through the back door.

There was no one else in the gambling hall except Lee's body and the bartender. Sawyer stared at the grim-faced man and made a violent motion of neutrality. He sent his still smoking Colt spinning down the bar and raised his hands to the top of his bald head.

His voice was tense. "I think Lee went a little

loco, fella. After he missed you, he turned on me." Sawyer gulped. "I had to shoot him."

"Where's Judge Selman?" Slade growled.

Sawyer licked his lips. "Rode out to Starlight. He bought a share in the ranch from Philip Canady last night!"

Slade felt the cold weight of this settle on him. He had left six men at the ranch — they might or might not fight. But he couldn't leave them to hold off Selman and his gun crew. Whatever happened now, he had tied himself to Arrant Canady's spread, and he had to see it through.

He walked across the empty gambling hall, his footsteps echoing in the stillness. He didn't look back at Sawyer, or at the man huddled at the base of the wall.

Matt was in Ma Crane's living room, slumped in a big chair. Tommy was running in and out of a doorway where his mother was packing. Laura came into the living room, her eyes searching Slade's bruised face.

Matt said with bad temper: "Where have you been?"

"Rode over to Siding," Slade growled. "I was due to pick up Martha Upton —"

"Who?" Matt's voice held a sneer.

Slade gripped his temper. He told them about the telegram, and why he had wanted to keep it secret. "It would have proved this man wasn't Philip Canady," he ended coldly. "I knew he

176

wasn't Philip anyway. I knew it the moment I saw him." He took a deep breath. "Because I knew Philip Canady as well as you did, Laura. Perhaps better — in some ways. I was Arrant's partner, on the old Pitchfork spread —"

Laura sank slowly down into a chair. Matt frowned. "You knew all along, yet you didn't speak up. You came here knowing Arrant had left half of Starlight to you — yet you didn't tell Laura that you knew this impostor wasn't Philip —"

"I didn't know Arrant had left me half of Starlight," Slade cut him off curtly. "I came to Starlight Basin to kill him. I arrived a few days too late —"

He saw Laura's face grow still. Her eyes were on him, asking her questions.

He told them why, about the year of paralysis — the long years of hate. "I'll never know why Arrant tried to kill me," he concluded. "But I saw him up on that ridge, just a glimpse, before he rode away. It couldn't have been anyone else."

Matt was looking at Laura; for a few seconds his jealousy showed in his face. Then he turned to Slade.

"Then Laura is legally entitled to a half-share in Starlight," he said. He smiled grimly. "You might try convincing her, Slade. She's packing to leave —"

"Yes." Laura's voice was still, flat. "I don't care any more. I don't want Starlight. So many people have been killed —" She buried her face in her hands.

"It wasn't your fault," Slade said. "And I wish you'd wait, at least until morning —"

"Why?" Matt's tone probed. "Why should she wait, Slade? She's got nothing here. And neither have you. Judge Selman rode out an hour ago. He's gone to take over Starlight —"

"I know," Slade said. But his eyes were on Laura, and his voice was hard with conviction. "Wait until tomorrow, Laura?"

She lifted her face. Something in his eyes, in his voice, reached through to her. She nodded slowly.

"I'll wait. . . ."

Chapter Sixteen

Willy Ames ran his thumb across the thick sheaf of bills Selman had paid him before putting them into his grip. Three thousand dollars wasn't much for a ranch like Starlight. But then, he reflected philosophically, it was a lot of money for the little work he had done. And anyway, he had been glad to get away from New Orleans —

He was reaching inside the dresser drawer for his shirts when a knock on his door startled him. The unexpected sound froze him, while his thoughts jumped to the grim-faced man who had told him to wait before selling to Selman.

If Walleye had failed to stop Slade, then his goose was cooked!

The knock came again, sharp and imperious.

Ames slid the .38 out of his underarm holster and slipped the pistol inside his coat pocket. He kept his fingers around it as he said with only a trace of annoyance: "Come in."

A girl came in, smiling, pushing the door shut behind her. "Surprise," she greeted. But her smile was not all welcome — it had a cold, calculating hardness.

"*Jeanne!*" He almost spat the word out. "I thought you were —"

"A thousand miles behind — in New Orleans. No?" Her voice was unpleasant. "You were clever, oh, so clever. But," her lips curled, "not as clever as you think, eh?"

His finger tightened on the trigger. He almost shot her before he realized that the shot would be heard. So far, barring what had occurred in New Orleans, he was in the clear with the law. He had a good chance of heading west, for California, and starting afresh. But if he killed this girl here . . .

"You theenk I do not not know, eh?" she was saying. "But I read the letters — the letters from Judge Selman of Badwater. A rancho for you to claim, with no reesk —"

"You fool!" he interrupted her. "I was going back for you. This job was dangerous. I didn't want you to get hurt. Can't you understand?"

"But *oui*," Jeanne said. "I understand perfectly. But why should not a wife follow her husband, eh?"

"*Wife?*"

She nodded happily. "I am Mrs. Philip Canady. So I tell the beeg man who meet me at Siding." She tilted her head coquettishly. "Geel Slade! A beeg man, Willy. He say he work for you —"

Ames was breathing heavily. "You mean you rode into town with Slade? You empty-headed little fool! He's boss of Starlight. He owns half of the big rancho you thought you'd cut yourself in for!"

Her eyes went round. "He owns Starlight?"

"Not all of it," Ames snapped. "Half of it!"

She shrugged. She walked into the room, tossed her scarf on the bed. She loosened her coat, threw it on the bed beside the scarf and turned, shaking long black hair loose from under her hat.

"You do not seem happy to see me, Weely!" she pouted. "I am Mrs. Philip Canady — the wife of a beeg ranchero. *Très* beeg," she said, widening her eyes innocently. "I asked questions of the station man at Siding. Even half will make us rich —"

"I don't own any part of Starlight!" the gambler bit out. "I sold out last night — to the judge!"

She turned on him, the smile fading from her big brown eyes. "Then you are the fool!" she sneered. "It was your ranch — half of it, anyway. You didn't have to sell. Let the judge talk. Who would have believed him?"

Ames moved toward her. "And get killed?" His lips twisted. "You should have stayed in New Orleans. I was through with you, you cheap little —"

She slapped his face. "I deed not come for only to be weeth you!" she flared. "But now you will split with me, or I will tell this man, this Slade, who you really are." She laughed. "You are afraid, eh? I see it in your face —"

His hand slipped out of his coat pocket holding the pistol. "I always said you had a big

181

mouth, Jeanne," he sneered.

She turned and ran for the door. Her voice shrilled out a wild scream before he overtook her, slammed the gun across her head.

She slumped against the framing, her fingers clawing at the wood. The gambler bent, lifted her unconscious form and dragged her to the bed. All he wanted was time to get to Siding. He had discarded the former plan of taking the stage to Rawlins. They wouldn't be looking for him in Siding. And once he got aboard that train, heading west —

He whirled as the door flung open; whirled to look into Slade's bruised, grim face.

Slade glanced at the girl lying slumped across the bed. Ames' eyes flicked wildly from the girl to the tall man moving into the room.

"You've got no right to break into a man's room," he blustered. "Not when he has company —"

Slade's smile was bleak. "Your wife?"

Ames licked his lips. He had shoved his pistol back into his pocket; his hand was still gripped around it. But he didn't dare use it.

"Yes." He thought fast. "I didn't want my father to know I had married. When that other woman lied about being married to Philip Canady —"

"She didn't lie," Slade said. He walked to the bed, looked down at Jeanne's face. A slight trickle of blood marked her left cheek.

"This the way you always treat your wife?" His

voice held a bleak sarcasm.

"How I treat my wife is no concern of yours," Ames snarled. "She slipped and fell. I was on my way out to get help —"

"Dr. Mays?"

"Mays is dead!" It slipped out from the gambler's lips, hard and curt.

"Of course," Gil nodded. "Doc Mays was killed because he was the only other person in town who knew that Martha Upton, Arrant Canady's Pitchfork housekeeper, was coming in yesterday on the noon train at Siding. She knew Philip Canady well. It would have spoiled everything, wouldn't it? So Selman sent a man to find out what Doc knew — and then he killed him. He sent a couple of men out to kill Martha and me, too —"

Jeanne stirred on the bed, moaned.

Ames shot her a glance. "I don't know what you're talking about, Slade!" he blustered. "I'm Philip Canady —"

"You're a liar!" Slade snapped. He faced Ames, his face hard. "I knew Philip well. I was Arrant Canady's partner on the old Pitchfork spread in Montana!"

Ames' eyes widened. "Slade! Yes, now I remember —"

"Sure you remember!" Slade snarled. "You'll have a long time to remember. I'm putting you under citizen's arrest, until we get some sort of law in Badwater —"

He caught the motion of the gambler's hand

inside his pocket and lunged away, his own Colt coming up in his hand. The blond man's .38 barked its spiteful message, the bullet raking a shallow cut across Slade's ribs.

The heavier blast of the .45 spun Ames around. He fell against the dresser and slid down, dazed, shocked by the impact of the bullet in his leg.

Slade stepped forward and pulled the pistol from the gambler's limp grasp.

He heard Jeanne gasp behind him. He turned and went to her. She was sitting up, clinging to the brass bedpost.

Slade pushed her hair away from her bruise and examined the cut scalp. "You'll be all right, Jeanne," he said. "A headache for a day or two —"

"Yes," she whispered. "I'll be all right." She looked down at Ames, hunched over his bullet-shattered thigh. The man was in a state of shock, bordering on unconsciousness. His breathing was heavy.

"He was a fool," she whispered. "He's not Philip Canady. He is Willy Ames, gambler and card sharp. He knew Philip Canady well — roomed with him. But Philip Canady is dead —"

"Thanks for telling me," Slade said. "I knew he wasn't Philip. And I suspected that the real Philip Canady was dead —" He looked at her. "And you — you're not Philip's wife?"

She shook her head. "I knew Philip, too. I didn't like him. He was — a boy." She fingered

184

the bruise over her temple, winced. "I am Jeanne DeVries. I danced in the Gay Paree in New Orleans. Walter Selman — he is called the judge here — knew Willy. He knew that Philip Canady was dead. He came here, after he and Willy read a clipping Philip had cut out of the paper. It was from his father, asking him to come home — to this ranch in Starlight Basin. Walter Selman came here first. Later he wrote to Willy. I read some of the letters. The last one asked Willy to come to Badwater to pose as Philip Canady."

Slade nodded. Selman's whole scheme had come apart — but Selman and his men were still to be reckoned with. On the frontier, possession was nine tenths of the law. And once Selman took over Starlight —

He handed Jeanne the .38 he had taken from Ames. "I don't think he's in any condition to go anywhere," he said dryly. "But just in case —"

"He'll be here," she said. She remembered the rasping insult with which he had lashed her. "I promise. . . ."

She sat on the bed after Slade left. Ames looked at her. "The money —" he whispered. "In my bag. Help me get out —"

He tried to get up. A sudden spasm went through him, and he fell back limply against the dresser.

Jeanne turned to the grip. She found the money where Ames had tucked it. The pain went out of her eyes. *"Mon Dieu!"* she whispered hap-

pily. "I have not made the long trip for nothing —"

Laura Canady was in Ma Crane's doorway
when she saw Slade ride by. Her eyes followed
him on the way out of town on the road to Starlight. She watched him for a long time, until he
faded against the cold whiteness. . . .

Slade could hear rifle firing long before he
came in sight of the ranch. He kept to Little
Timber Creek, which provided cover as he
approached Starlight. A half-mile from the
ranch yard he dismounted, left his roan con-
cealed in a thicket.

The firing seemed to come from two places:
from behind the barn, which faced the galley and
the ranch-house across the yard; and from the
galley.

There was a lull in the firing as he neared. The
judge's sharp voice rang out: "Nelson! Don't be
a pigheaded fool! You and the rest of the boys
come out with your hands on your heads and
we'll let you ride out of here. You have my word
for it!"

Nelson's voice had a mocking defiance. "You
know what you can do with yore word, Judge!"

Slade reached the side of the barn away from
the Crescent gunmen without being seen. As he
started for the corner he heard Selman's bitter
voice say: "We'll have to burn the fools out! I
didn't want to do it. But now I want every one of
those stubborn fools shot —"

Slade stepped around the side of the barn. "It's going to be a little hotter this side of hell, Judge!"

The boss of Crescent whirled. Cramer and two others Slade had not seen before flanked him. Ten feet away, just beginning to crawl under the nearest corral bars, was Pete Cajun. The half-breed stiffened, turning to stare with beady eyes at the rangy newcomer.

The judge glanced at the rifle in Slade's hand. He was holding a rifle himself — Cramer, Eames and Sellers had Colts. For a stark violent moment after Slade's flat announcement no one moved.

Then Selman jerked his rifle up, jerking the trigger prematurely, firing before the muzzle leveled. Slade's slug doubled him. Slade's second shot tore through Cramer's throat, pinning him momentarily against the side of the barn.

Cajun rolled and managed to flick a knife at Slade before Slade's bullet smashed between his ribs.

Sellers and Eames didn't move. Faces white, they dropped their Colts and raised their hands.

Sellers said: "Count us out, Slade!"

Slade nodded. "Arch!" he called, lifting his voice. "You can come out now. It's all over!"

Willy Ames, along with Sellers and Eames, was held in the Badwater jail until the law could take charge from Rawlins. The veterinarian from Siding came to town to doctor Ames' smashed thigh, and for a while it seemed the gambler might die.

He was gaunt and still a very sick man when the deputy from Rawlins came for him. Slade was there; he had written his testimony and handed it to the deputy and promised he'd be in Rawlins for the trial.

Ames said: "You never liked Philip Canady, did you, Slade?"

Slade looked at him. "No," he said slowly. "I didn't like him."

Ames said: "He hated you, hated you like poison. He was the one who shot you, you know —"

Slade was by the door. He stood very still, while the deputy looked at him, frowned, and looked at the gambler.

"He told me about it one night: how he rode out after you, shot you. His father had followed him. Arrant near killed him that night, he said. That's when he ran away —"

Slade's face twitched. *Five years of hating the wrong man —*

He saw the sneer on Ames' face, but it didn't mean anything to him. He turned and left the room and went outside into the cold, clear day.

Laura Canady was waiting for him at Ma Crane's. She was packed, and he had taken the buckboard to town. Reverend Smith had promised to come over to Starlight at two o'clock sharp.

It was to be a simple wedding.

As he stepped up into the seat of the buck-board, Slade wondered if Arrant Canady was sorry. . . .